THIN BLUE LINE

Thin Blue Line

ISBN: 978-1-7348524-4-8 (hardback)
978-1-7348524-5-5 (paperback)
978-1-7348524-6-2 (ebook)

Printed in the United States of America

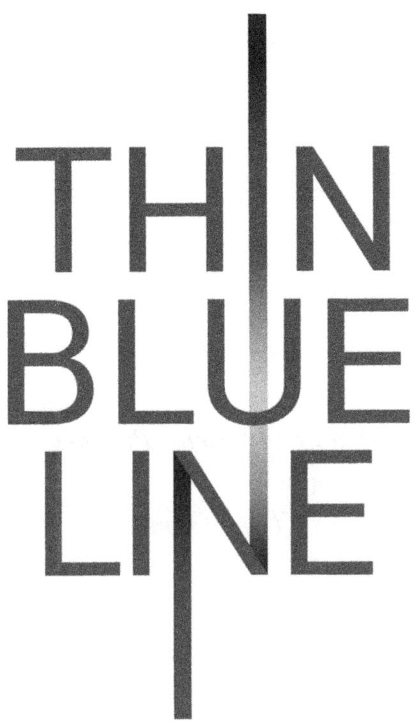

A Jeannie Loomis Novel

GARY J. ROSE

TITLES BY GARY J. ROSE

JEANNIE LOOMIS NOVELS

Ark of the Covenant – Raid on the Church of Our Lady Mary of Zion

Star Chamber

Forgotten Plans

House of Special Purpose

Time Game

NON-FICTION

Towards the Integration of Police Psychology Techniques to Combat Juvenile Delinquency in K-12 Classrooms

How to Create a Military Style Boot Camp Academy in Public Schools

Teaching Inside the Walls

To Mom

Mike Lake

Jane and Fred Vallier
(Vallier Communications)

Crime had become epidemic in San Francisco. Gangs fought over drug turfs--leaving corpses in their wakes and overwhelming the San Francisco Police Department as the homicide rate increased.

Before officers could stem the tide of violence, they became the targets. A cop killer was on the loose, and the police turned to the San Francisco bureau of the FBI and Special Agent Jeannie Loomis and her team for help

CHAPTER ONE

Officer Ronnie Grayson liked his part-time job at Donuts and Mud, the Millennial version of the once national fast food chain, Winchell's Donuts. He fondly remembers when his dad used to share cop-talk, or what they called "wargames," with fellow officers who stopped by after his retirement to shoot the shit. Now retired after a thirty-year career on the force, he was paying the price for eating all those donuts over the years--a recently quadruple bypass.

Grayson followed in his shoes and chose a career in law enforcement, joining the SFPD four and a half years earlier. He took the part-time security guard job at the donut shop because he needed money as a part-time law school student attending Golden Gate University Law School. The department allowed him to wear his SFPD uniform while on the job, hoping it would discourage robberies. It had become common practice to allow uniformed officers to moonlight as security officers, especially during the recent escalation in crime. Businesses, customers, and employees alike felt more secure in their presence.

On this particular day he sat in his customary seat, a booth facing the entrance to the shop. Studying the subject of Torts and Contracts on his laptop, he did not notice the African American walk up to the front glass façade. No one inside saw the dark figure of a person firing three rapid shots into the establishment until they saw him run and disappear into the darkness and fog that had descended onto San Francisco streets. Two bullets grazed the back of Grayson's neck.

He peered into the darkness to see if he could see the shooter and radioed for assistance, not knowing the shots origin or if the gunman were still outside waiting to take additional shots.

Responding officers raced to the scene, but the gunman was nowhere in sight. There was no robbery attempt; it appeared the shooter's sole purpose was to kill the seated officer.

Based on limited witness accounts, the police felt the shooter acted alone. The forensic team found three 9mm shell casings outside on the sidewalk, and slugs found in the donut shop walls confirmed they came from a semi-automatic.

Although Officer Grayson survived the shooting with only minor injuries, officers later targeted by the gunman would not be so lucky.

Less than three weeks later, a hooded figure stood in an alleyway across from a bar frequented by law enforcement officers. When he felt the time was right, he entered with a weapon in his right hand and fired ten rounds before the officers could react. Three individuals were hit in an instant. One was a police sergeant and the other two were federal agents. All three died at the scene. Again, the shooter was shrouded by San Francisco fog and disappeared.

Sometime during the night, Jeannie in a half-awake, half-dream like state was thinking about her life. A self-examination confirmed she was a mid-forties female, not bad-looking--if she could brag to herself--divorced twice, childless, and the Assistant Special Agent in Charge with the Federal Bureau of Investigation in San Francisco. At the time, she was not dating and still coping with the loss of her fiancé, Ricky Pinheiro, who was killed by urban terrorists. Jeannie felt that things could only get better going forward.

Jeannie was startled by the ringtone of her cellphone. Before answering, she looked at her alarm clock. It was 1:18 a.m. No one can expect good news from a call at that hour, she thought. It had to be the bureau. "Loomis," she said, waiting for the bad news. Sure enough, she was informed that three officers had been fatally shot at a cop bar in the "City By The Bay's" Mission District. One was an FBI agent that reported to Jeannie. Of the other two, one was a federal agent of the U.S. Department of Fish and Wildlife, and the other was a patrol sergeant from the San Francisco Police Department.

Initially, she could not put a face to the FBI agent's name since several agents had been recently transferred in due to the FBI's shake-up coming from D.C.; house cleaning was still underway from the corruption fallout at the bureau's top. Fortunately, Jeannie was able to stay under the radar and continue her climb up the promotion ladder. The fallen agent's name was Michael Atwood, a 32-year-old husband and father-to-be.

Jeannie requested dispatch to notify her partner, Special Agent Ismail Flores, and have him meet her at the bar where the shooting occurred. Whenever possible, Jeannie liked to visit crime scenes and take in the environment, smells, and anything else that might help her analyze her gut feelings--which she felt most successful officers use to solve crimes.

Jeannie Loomis was a seventeen-year veteran of the FBI, rapidly climbing the ranks which had previously been male-heavy at the top. After surviving a shooting in one of their satellite offices and consequently losing her unborn child, she was offered the SAC job in San Francisco but opted to take the Assistant position to learn the ropes. She was successful in arranging the transfer of her co-worker, friend, and confidant--Special Agent Ismail Flores--and two topnotch IT specialists, Darcy and Burk who would join her.

She and her team had recently solved an armored car robbery-turned-homicide case, taking down four suspects. After Jeannie took over the director reins of a serial killer task force in Marin County, she and her team successfully captured the elusive Daniel Koufax.

However, all of these investigations took a backseat to their case involving the notorious Joey, former leader of the Sons and Daughters of Liberty, an assassination squad that eliminated individuals found guilty by the secret Star Chamber Court. After kidnapping the teenage daughter of a wealthy high-tech company owner, employing tactics similar to those used by the SLA in the 1970s, the Sons and Daughters of Liberty killed Jeannie's fiancé in a Concord, California shootout.

Joey, who did not participate in the shootout, followed up by placing canisters holding the deadly Marburg virus in the Los Angeles Convention Center's air-conditioning ducts, hoping to infect Democratic National Convention attendees. Acting swiftly, Jeannie and her team removed the deadly virus before it could be released and took Joey into custody as he was leaving the United States. He later died at the hands of fellow prison inmates.

The Elbow Room Bar located at 647 Valencia Street was initially home to the city's landmark lesbian bar, Amelia's, which opened in the 1970s and operated through the late 1980s. The building is a two-story structure with the main bar located downstairs; a secondary bar adjoins the dance floor and stage upstairs. The club caters to a wide range of musical tastes. On any given night, live bands and DJs play rock, hip-hop, soul, metal, indie, and a little punk. Cops tend to hangout on the first floor where the shootings took place.

Jeannie parked her Vette near the taped off area behind Ismail's bureau Crown Vic. "Hey, Ace," she said when she saw Ismail near the entrance. "How bad is it?"

"It's not a drive-by. This cold-blooded motherfucker walked into the bar and fired off at least five or more rounds, then walked out. It was a deliberate attack," Ismail said. "My gut tells me it won't be this guy's last."

"Any idea who he targeted?" Jeannie asked.

"Too early to tell, but I guess we can't rule out anything at this point. It could just be a bunch of cops trying to release some stress after work and some random shooter opened up on them. On the other hand, it could be that one of those hit was the target, and the others were just collateral damage. Who knows?" Ismail replied.

"OK. I've already requested that our Chaplin meet me at Atwood's home in Oakland. You stay here while forensic does their thing and see if we have any more to work with. After I meet with Atwood's wife, I'll meet you at the bureau and we can review everything," Jeannie said as she started walking to her vehicle, dreading what might lie ahead when she makes the death notification.

"I don't envy you, boss," said Ismail. "Sure you don't want me to tag along?"

"No, thanks for the offer," she replied. "The Chaplin and I should have it under control. If you feel a need for more manpower, go ahead and call them in. The media will be all over this by tomorrow morning.

CHAPTER TWO

As the morning was giving way to noontime, the drive to Oakland seemed to take forever. Jeannie didn't remember the drive across the Oakland-San Francisco Bay Bridge or the climb up the foothills overlooking the city. There was nothing Jeannie liked about Oakland. It had a high crime rate and homeless encampments had popped up everywhere. It seemed to be a mirror of San Francisco without the views. She remembered something that Joey, the now-dead urban terrorists of the Sons and Daughters of Liberty, said while she and her team pursued the elusive mastermind. "One thing all these cities have in common," he said, "was that they were all managed by Democrats."

Trying to keep her mind off of the unpleasant task before her, Jeannie had to agree with Joey. Think of all the cities now under duress--riots, fires, mayhem, shootings, murder in Philadelphia, Chicago, Minneapolis, San Francisco, Los Angeles, Portland,

Seattle, and on-and-on--all managed by a Democratic mayor or governor, or both.

She had no problem finding the address. It was a nice house given the neighborhood, and she wondered how one of her agents could afford such an upscale residence.

I need to investigate this later, she thought. As she prepared to get out of her car, she received a text saying the Chaplain had also just arrived. She saw parking lights reflect off another parked car and saw the Chaplain exit her vehicle, a Ford Mustang. Shelly Wilcox saw Jeannie when she got out of her car, waved and walked toward her. "Sorry for your loss," Shelly said.

"Thanks. But to be honest with you, he was a new transfer, so I don't know anything about him. I'm so glad you were free to meet me here. I hate these things, but more so when I don't feel I have anything to contribute," Jeannie replied.

"I understand completely. If you introduce yourself and me and explain what happened, I can take over. Most of the death notices I have to make are about individuals I don't know. I hate to say it, but we have a well-rehearsed narrative that all of us Chaplains use in such circumstances. The main thing we have to avoid is coming across as a robot."

The house was dark, but the exterior had outdoor lighting. Jeannie rang the doorbell and she and Shelly waited for several minutes. At first, they thought that perhaps no one was at home, but finally they heard footsteps coming toward the front door and the porch light came on. Jeannie could see movement behind the door's peephole followed by a female voice saying hello. Jeannie took a deep breath and identified herself, raising her identification to the peephole.

"Oh my God!" she screamed. "Is Mike alright?" she asked while removing a security chain and unlocking the door. Mrs. Atwood was wearing a bathrobe that did little to conceal her pregnancy. Her hair showed she had been sleeping. "It's about Mike. Is he alright?" she asked again. Jeannie requested that she and Shelly enter the residence. Once instead, but before sitting, Jeannie formally introduced herself.

"Your Mike's supervisor, right?" she asked.

"Yes, and this is Shelly Wilcox." Jeannie did not identify Wilcox as a Chaplain. Mrs. Atwood, maybe we should all sit down."

"Yes, yes. I'm sorry, please have a seat," Mrs. Atwood said while pointing to a couch. Please, call me Marsha."

"Marsha," Jeannie said. "There was a shooting tonight at a bar in San Francisco. Three individuals were shot, and one was your husband." Marsha began to cry and placed her hand over her unborn child. "I'm so sorry. Mike didn't make it."

"No. You have to be wrong. Mike and I are having a baby. He can't be dead. I think you have him mixed up with someone else. Mike promised he'd always wear a bullet-proof vest. No. Mike is fine. He called me and told me he'd have a drink with Rob at some bar in the city. Rob works undercover for the Federal Fish and Wildlife Department. Rob would have called me if Mike got hurt."

At this point, the Chaplin took over. Jeannie could not recall on her drive back across the bay if Shelly eventually identified her position or not.

Jeannie began having flashbacks of being notified by the surgeon of her fiancé Ricky Pinheiro's death. She caught herself tearing up and had to wipe her eyes with the cuff of her long-sleeved blouse. She loved her job except for moments like these; but fortunately for her, they were few and far between. Even though the SFPD was being crushed with an overwhelming increase in violent crimes--one homicide a day--they had not affected the bureau per se until now. It was about to get even worse.

CHAPTER THREE

While during the early morning hours when a gunman was opening fire on unsuspecting law enforcement officers relieving stress in the Elbow Room Bar, a serial killer was again about to perform a ritual inside a turn-of-the-century farmhouse 62 miles south of San Francisco in San Jose, California--home of the San Jose Sharks hockey team, the famous "haunted" Winchester Mystery House, Silicon Valley, and orchard and farmland rich foothills--and only 36 miles north of Santa Cruz and its beaches.

The killer knew the configuration of the house and site well enough; he spent two weeks laboring in the hot sun picking apricots for the owners. They paid well, and he could not complain about that. But he knew they had even more money and it was stored on the premises. Peering through a window, he saw the old man put cash in a safe housed in a spare bedroom.

"This morning I will make my offering to my God, who will make sure my mama and papa spend eternity

in hell," he thought, slowing down his bike and looking for the large bush he remembered abutting the rear of the home. The bush and limited light from the quarter moon helped conceal him. Seeing no lights on in the house, he freed two bungee cords holding his instrument of death on the rear of his bike. Approaching a bedroom window he already knew was not the master, he felt his hip to make sure the hunting knife was still in its sheath.

The window's putty was chipped and dry. *Easy to remove*, he thought. Pulling out the knife, he began working on the window. Disturbing thoughts entered his mind--all-consuming thoughts of his father placing a chain around his throat and attaching it to a post, the hot Mexican sun beating down on his nude body, his father raising the bullwhip and bringing it down with increasing severity each time. He could remember feeling the blood run down his back, and the lashes reaching his face, unleashing rivers of blood that entered his mouth, his father laughing each time a blow was landed; and there by his side, his mother who had been told by her husband to not look away.

When the beatings stopped, physical torture turned to psychological torture as his father placed a dog dish filled with water just beyond his reach. He would remain there for hours until his papa gave his mama permission to remove the chain.

And his mother--what did she do to ease his torment? Nothing. Finally, she would remove the chain and point to the water dish. Sometimes the whipping was so severe that he had to crawl to the water dish, and yet his mama did not help. The same mother that had given him birth and provided him with breast milk had become his papa's accomplice.

This night, his offerings would continue their banishment to hell. Killing his parents while they slept a night long ago only gave temporary relief from his thirst for revenge.

Easing himself through the window, he lowered himself into the spare bedroom and listened for the sound of someone awake. Hearing none, he grabbed his tool and began walking down the dark hallway. Using his left hand, he followed the wall down the hallway to his victims' room--victims that would be offered to his God in a blood sacrifice using Santeria rituals.

The old man was sleeping on his back. *An easy attack*, the intruder thought. Reciting chants silently to himself, he raised the tool over his head and brought it down with thunderous speed. A crushing sound filled the room, but the female next to him did not stir. He tried to pull the tool free, but it would not give. He climbed onto the bed and began moving the tool back and forth, up and down, finally freeing it. The old lady awakened, began to scream and tried to raise herself from her pillow. He raised the tool once again and hit her on the crown of her head. Again, the sound of crushing bone filled the bedroom. They were both dead. He was sure of that.

He returned his attention to the old man who now looked like his papa. Rage filled his body and he raised the tool again and again, smashing his "father's" face. He turned to his "mother" and repeated blows to her body as well.

He pulled back the bedcover and top sheet, and pulled his "father's" pajama pants down. Grabbing the shriveled old penis surrounded by gray hair, he pulled out his hunting knife. A few cuts, and his "father" was no longer a man.

And you, Mama," he said out loud to himself. "You who stood by and watched while he whipped me and abused me. You who breast fed me. You were never a mother. You do not need these." He began cutting at her right breast. After removing both breasts, he moved to her eyes. "Mother, you do not need these eyes. You did not see when papa whipped me? You could not see when he came into my bedroom at night. I cried out to you, but you never came to see what was wrong. No Mother, your eyes are not important to you."

CHAPTER FOUR

Jeannie arrived at her office as SAC (Special Agent in Charge) Lomax was leaving the breakroom with a fresh cup of coffee. "Heard you had an early morning. How did the death notification go?" he asked, having done many himself over the course of his career, and not really expecting or wanting an answer.

"Thank God Shelly Wilcox was on-call. She carried most of the burden. What hurt me the most was that I never really met Michael. I was so tied up with the serial killer task force, and then with the armored car robbery that I never had time to sit down and talk with him. Hell, I never even looked at his file," Jeannie said while unlocking her office door and entering.

Lomax took a seat opposite Jeannie. Neither said anything. Lomax broke the silence. "Look, for what it's worth, I did have coffee with Michael after he transferred here. He was part of the house cleaning effort conducted by Washington. He confided in me that he was very glad to get transferred out of D.C. and relocated to the bay area with his pregnant wife. He called D.C. a cesspool, and I couldn't agree more. He said that the bureau's higher ranks were so corrupt with hatred for the president that he almost left the bureau out of disgust. Did you know his great-grandfather was an agent under J. Edgar Hoover, himself, back in the Al Capone era? Listening to his grandfather's many relived stories prompted him to wear the badge."

Agent Ismail Flores, Jeannie's senior agent, saw Lomax sitting across from her and knocked before entering. "If I'm interrupting…" he said, but Lomax stood, patted Ismail on the shoulder before receiving an answer and left Jeannie's office. "Tough day for everyone around here, huh!" he commented.

"That's an understatement. So, what do we have on the shootings?" Jeannie asked Ismail.

"Appears to have been a single shooter. We found numerous 9mm shell casings. A preliminary forensics review failed to show prints. Looks like he fired ten rounds. According to witnesses, he entered the bottom floor bar with the gun in his hand and didn't walk very far inside. Apparently looking at no one in particular, he opened fire until he ran out of bullets, turned and left. Cool, calm, and collected. Could be a pro, but since he didn't seem focused on any one particular person--I don't know. Maybe he's ex-military."

"Any surveillance tapes?" Jeannie asked.

"Only from outside the bar, but because of the thick fog they're worthless. I've already given the tapes to Darcy and Burk to see if they can clean them up, but I doubt it can be done. This is going to be a who-done-it," Ismail replied.

CHAPTER FIVE

Three days later at 2:15 a.m., and only six blocks from the SFPD (San Francisco Police Department) Richmond Station, officer Matt Riley, a 26-year-old and six-year veteran of the force, was writing up a report inside his patrol vehicle. Using his dash-mounted lamp, he was quickly checking all the boxes on his computer, hoping his sergeant would not kick it back later as incomplete. Usually, he would have just kissed off the incident he investigated as a family fight with no one wanting to press charges; but with all the domestic violence crap, he now needed to cover his ass with a report. A taxicab was double-parked on the opposite side of the street. Officer Riley looked at the cab, but did not see anyone enter or exit, nor was it illuminated. He continued working on his report.

He didn't hear or see a man approach his cruiser, raise his hand and fire four times into Riley's body at close range--hitting his, neck, and shoulder. Somehow

Riley was able to struggle out of his patrol car and fire off two rounds at the fleeing male suspect before falling to his knees, and then face-first to the ground.

The cab driver, Mahmood Abass, witnessed the shooting and quickly contacted his dispatcher, describing the suspect's escape route. Remaining on the line with the dispatcher, he circled the block to see if he could track the shooter.

The gunman ran into an alleyway, discarding his hoodie and black ski mask as he fled to change his appearance. Turning the corner at the end of block, the cabbie saw the shooter emerge from the alley. "I got him. I got him," he told his dispatcher as the shooter hailed the cab to stop. Before stopping, he told his dispatcher that the lift was the shooter.

Not realizing the cabbie had witnessed the shooting and before the driver could react, the assailant climbed into the back seat. The cabbie discreetly turned off his radio and focused on the black male now sitting in his cab. The gunman assumed various positions as if looking to see if he were being followed. He was wearing black leather gloves that exposed half of his fingers and his right hand held a semi-automatic. Unknown to him, the dispatcher was simultaneously contacting the SFPD. The shooter did not give the cabbie a final destination, only instructions to drive straight or make turns.

SFPD put out a BOLO (be on the lookout) for cab number 662 which was also being tracked by an onboard GPS device. The driver tried to remain calm, knowing the police were trying to discretely find his cab. Within minutes, SFPD Officer Stan Alshire pulled behind the cab. The shooter saw the patrol unit and placed his gun against Mahmood's head, barking out an address. Another patrol unit joined the first. Mahmood made a right turn and very suddenly slammed on the brakes.

The gunman, startled by the abrupt stop, kicked open the back door, bolted out of the cab, accidently dropped his weapon on the ground, and fled into the neighborhood--evading the pursuing officers. The officers retrieved the weapon which had only six 9 mm bullets--four less than a fully-loaded clip. Backup officers searched the area, but the gunman had disappeared.

At the crime scene, Officer Riley was fighting for his life as he was placed on a gurney and rushed to the hospital. Remarkably, he survived emergency surgery that removed four bullets. Forensic team members in the alley photographed the entire area before tagging and bagging the shooter's discarded hoodie and black ski mask.

Jeannie was lost in thought at her desk when the phone rang. It was SAC Lomax.

"Jeannie, there's been another cop shooting in the city. I don't know if there's any connection to the bar shooting, but I told SFPD we'd send someone over to see what they have and to compare notes. It happened around two in the morning, but they still have the scene locked down. If you and Ismail are free, I'd like the two of you to run over there."

Jeannie rode with Ismail, the Richmond Station giving them directions to the first crime scene where Officer Riley was shot. The forensic team assigned to the location was just finishing. Detective Tom Hanson saw the two agents identifying themselves to the officer behind the crime scene tape and approached them. After a brief greeting and handshakes, he told Jeannie and Ismail what they already surmised.

Not getting much information at that location, they headed to crime scene number two, following Detective Hanson's directions to the site. The forensic team had completed their investigation there and left, but two uniformed officers remained.

"Male, black. About 25-30 years old. 5'9" to 6'1." Average build. Clean shaven. Short hair. Calm and cool according to the cabbie," Officer Sally Yates said while her partner, Sam Prescot listened. "He probably jumped several fences and was out of here before we could conduct a thorough search. Couldn't use the chopper due to the fog. No one saw or heard anything, or they don't want to get involved," she added.

Concluding they got all the information they could at the two crime scenes, Jeannie and Ismail returned to the bureau. While each were getting a cup of coffee,

Jeannie's receptionist tracked her down and told her the SAC wanted to see her when she got back. "I'll catch up with you later," Ismail said as he headed to the bathroom.

Jeannie picked up her While-U-Were-Out messages and walked down the hallway to Lomax's office. She found him talking on the phone, sitting with his back to the door. From what she overhead, she surmised he was talking to a higher-up at a police agency, but he concluded the call before she could surmise its nature.

"I know you want to hunt for your cop killer, Jeannie, but Washington has requested that you assist the San Jose Police Department with a serial killer case they may have. I guess your behavior analysis skills are known throughout this wacko state we call California. Now, before you voice your objection, let me tell you what they have up to this point." Jeannie took a deep breath and put her messages on Lomax's desk, knowing the decision had already been made.

"I just got off the phone with Captain Williams of the San Jose Police Department. They have a vicious killer on the loose in the southern part of the city who's heading down to Morgan Hill and Gilroy. His hunting grounds appear to be rural undeveloped areas. This son-of-a-bitch preys on the elderly and the weak, and apparently there's a lot of overkill involved.

"His M.O. (modus operandi) appears to be gaining entrance into their homes and attacking them as they sleep. After his third kill, they realized they had a serial killer on their hands. Not making any headway on their own, they contacted our BAU (Behavioral Analysis Unit) in Quantico who provided their perspective of his behavior and possible motivation. Nevertheless, Bill--Captain Williams--has heard about your role as task force director in the Marin County serial and he's requesting your help. He warned me there's a lot of politics going on in the department and wanted you to be aware. Not as if we here don't have any, huh?"

Jeannie knew that Lomax was not a fan of whining, so she did not object to aiding the SJPD. "OK, I can leave Ismail and the team to work on our case. Do you have Captain William's phone number? I'll give him a call. It's not like television, is it?" she asked.

"What do you mean?" he asked.

"In a television show the whole God damned BAU would jump in a private jet and fly out to the requesting agency."

"I see what you mean. Sadly, here we put our best agent in a red Corvette and send her on her way. Good luck. Make me proud."

CHAPTER SIX

"Hey Ace, I'm afraid I have to leave you in charge again. San Jose P.D. feels they have a serial killer and they've requested my assistance," Jeannie said.

"Gee, I'm telling you ladies and gentlemen, we have a celebrity right here in our midst," Ismail said, finishing his coffee and suppressing a laugh to an empty breakroom.

"Hilarious, asshole!" she responded. "Don't mess up my office while I'm gone--and no, you can't keep my car. It's not a perk that goes with the job."

"Bummer. I was hoping to take the wifey for a spin in your Vette and maybe getting lucky afterwards," Ismail quipped.

"You know, that could be perceived as sexual harassment or something in today's politically correct society," Jeannie responded with a smile.

"No, my wife loves it. I'm the one being harassed. She can't keep her hands off me," Ismail retorted.

"Right. You need to see the shrink and get that narcissistic personality disorder of yours checked out," she said laughing. "I'll give you a check-in call tonight to see how your case is going and give you an update on the latest in San Jose."

"Be safe," he said as Jeannie left the breakroom and headed to the secured garage area.

After calling Captain Williams and setting up a meeting time for later that afternoon, Jeannie drove home to pack an overnight bag in case she had to stay in the south-bay city longer than expected. San Jose is California's third-largest city, only outdone by Los Angeles and San Diego. It is surrounded by the rolling hills of Silicon Valley and San Francisco Bay's southern shore to the north, and it is the major technology hub of the Bay Area. Its population hovers around a little more than a million, but swells with employees commuting into the area during the workweek to perform high-tech jobs. Besides being located within a booming high-tech industry area, San Jose is a cultural, political, and economic center that has earned the nickname, "Capital of Silicon Valley." Major global tech companies including Cisco Systems, eBay, Adobe Inc, PayPal, Broadcom, Samsung, Acer, Hewlett Packard, and Zoom house their headquarters there.

Living in San Jose is not much cheaper than the rest of the bay area, although the farther south one goes, the more affordable living costs become. Jeannie knew that the average home was over a million dollars, and for that one can expect a home manufactured in the 1950s during the baby boom; it is the fifth most expensive housing market in the world.

Jeannie's long deceased dad used to discuss San Jose 's transformation during their extended family drives to Watsonville, farther south on the coast. San Jose was initially divided into downtown, central, and western sections. As the population grew, people began referring to North, South, East, and West San Jose areas. Many of these regions were originally unincorporated communities or separate municipalities later annexed by the city. Like all large cities, there are good areas and areas to avoid if possible.

Jeannie was very familiar with the San Jose area, having driven there many times by herself or with friends as she got older. She knew that the city covered over 180 square miles, so the killer's hunting ground was huge. She had also visited the famed Winchester Mystery House several times, not to be amused by the tour guides' tales about the "haunted house" and its ghostly inhabitants, but to admire the house's craftsmanship and construction.

In the 1970s, Whites made up over 98% of the population, but that fell in the 21st century to only 42%. Now, almost 60% of the population is comprised of Hispanics and Asians, with only 3% Black. *It will be interesting to see if the San Jose Police Department has any witnesses who could give us the perps nationality,* Jeannie thought as she navigated Highway 101traffic. Finally, she arrived at 121 West Mission Street, the San Jose Police Department, parked her bureau car on the street and fed the parking meter. In San Francisco she could leave her Vette in the bureau's secured garage.

She knew the PD had almost one-thousand officers; however, fewer than the San Francisco PD. Although she had never met Captain Williams, she knew a few of the detectives at the department from when she taught a Behavioral Analysis class at Evergreen College. She found them very professional and highly trained, and with that in mind she wondered why she had been requested. Certainly, they had enough collective experience in the department to track down this killer.

She checked herself in the rear view mirror. Dressed in a dark blue business suit and silk bouse of the same color, she felt confident of making a good first impression. She showed her ID at the front counter and informed the duty officer that Captain Williams was expecting her. She took a seat in the lobby area, but before she had time to sort through a stack of old magazines to pass the time, she heard a buzzer and a tall male appeared wearing a SJPD uniform with two gold bars on the collar. "Agent Loomis, I'm glad to meet you," he said, offering his hand.

"Please, call me Jeannie," she said in friendly manner. After greetings were exchanged, Williams invited her to follow him toward his office, chatting as they went.

"How was the drive down from the city? I have to tell you, I hate driving up 101 to San Francisco these days. When I was a kid, it was a thrill to see Alcatraz, the bridges, and the Painted Ladies--I think that's what those old houses are called."

"You're right. They're called the Painted Ladies. The craftsmanship is outstanding. Have you ever gone inside one of them on a tour? Jeannie asked.

"No, and like I said, I try to avoid the City-by-the-Bay at all costs. It's sad to see what the city has become. No offense."

"None taken," Jeannie responded. "Most of the agents I work with feel the same way."

On the way to his office, they stopped at the breakroom where Jeannie was offered coffee. She turned that down, but asked for directions to the restroom. Williams was waiting when she returned, and they continued to his large office.

"Jeannie, this is the most brutal, cold-blooded killer I've ever investigated, and I'm going on thirty-years on the force. He's not satisfied with just killing individuals, each act is an act of overkill and mayhem. It's as if he goes into a frenzy after his victims are already dead. The fact that most of his victims are elderly and frail doesn't seem to affect the bastard at all. He's a cold-blooded sociopath. He doesn't take a backseat to Richard Ramirez, the Night Stalker, you know, in the mid-80s. I think when you meet with the other detectives and they tell you what we have, you'll note a lot of similarities to that case."

CHAPTER SEVEN

Jeannie was introduced to Lieutenant Farnsworth, but did not have time to review details of the killings since other homicide detectives began arriving early, partially out of curiosity about the new FBI agent that would be directing the task force. The room was much bigger than the one at the bureau in San Francisco. Farnsworth showed Jeannie several San Jose Mercury newspaper headline pages lying on the table near the podium. The media had attached a moniker for the killer--the San Jose Mutilator. As usual, no matter how diligent an agency tried to suppress information about a killing case, it got out. In this case they somehow heard that the killer took time to mutilate his victims' bodies. She was about to learn what other things he did.

The briefing room was on the second floor of the police department. When Jeannie entered, she glanced around and acknowledged several other detectives she recognized, but could not recall by name. Obviously, they were students she had taught in one of the numerous training sessions she offered in the bay area. She heard someone whisper about how good looking she was. "*You still got it girl,*" she thought to herself.

Captain Williams entered the room followed by a person who seemed to expect respect. *Has to be the new chief,* Jeannie thought. Sure enough, Captain Williams introduced her to the chief who said he was happy to have her and her experience as part of his department, and encouraged her to ask for anything she needed. As he finished, turned and walked out of the room, Jeannie thought she heard someone say, "Get the fuck out of here, prick." *Politics indeed,* Jeannie thought.

Jeannie looked in the direction of Lt. Farnsworth who had a hard time hiding his distaste for the chief. She knew that all law enforcement departments, especially larger ones, had internal politics that drove divisions. Considering the strife experienced by the FBI at the time, she understood the tension she sensed during the chief's brief presence.

Seventeen people were present, not counting Jeannie who was escorted to the front where several chairs had been placed behind a podium. She recalled a similar layout when she arrived the first time and met with the Marin County Sheriff's Department on the Koufax serial killer case. Jeannie quickly tried to compose something in her head in case she was called upon to speak.

"OK, take a seat ladies and gentlemen. We have a lot to cover, so let's get started," Captain Williams began, waiting for everyone to find a seat. He continued, "As you're aware, I requested the F.B.I. to allow Agent Jeannie Loomis of their San Francisco bureau to assist us in our serial killer case. As you can see," looking at Jeannie, "our request was granted.

"We're all aware of Agent Loomis and her team's success the last several years, the most recent being the arrest of Daniel Koufax in Marin County. I want to say without reservation that Agent Loomis' SAC assures me she's one of us and will back us up. There's no ego involved with her. She, like you, wants to catch our killer as soon as possible using both our resources and those of the FBI. Agent Loomis, would you like to say a few words before we give you a review of our case?"

Since it more of a request than a question, Jeannie stood and approached the podium. "First, I recognize a lot of you, but I guess I'm getting old and can't remember names like I used to. So, I apologize up front for not calling you by name." Most in the audience smiled, but she heard a few laugh. "Please come up later and introduce yourself, and I promise I'll try to remember your name this time. I want to thank Captain Williams for asking me to help you track down this vicious killer. As I told Lt. Farnworth, the taskforce members' grunt work made it possible to capture Koufax. I like to use the analogy of you being the team and I'm just the quarterback. As in football, it takes both a strong offense and defense. That's what Marin County had. We caught him because we worked as a team. I hope we'll do the same this time. But, enough about me, I really want to see what we're up against." She turned and walked back to her seat.

Captain Williams asked a female detective sitting near a computer to get the presentation set up, and motioned for Jeannie to join him in a couple of vacant first row seats. As the lights dimmed, Lt. Farnsworth, acting as the narrator in synch with the detective operating the computer and projector, started to review the killings.

"The first killings occurred on May ninth. At nine forty-seven in the morning, SJPD officer James Logan, a four-year veteran of the force, stopped at his elderly parent's house just inside our city limits to check on them. His sister phoned him, concerned that they hadn't returned her phone calls." A slide showed the outside of the Logan residence, an older farm-style house, probably built in the 1900's Jeannie thought, with a wooden façade including cedar shingles and planter boxes under the front windows. Jeannie could see that the day the picture was taken, the wooden framed screen door was held open by a rock, apparently so technicians and police could more easily pass through.

Lt. Farnsworth continued. "Officer Logan climbed the three porch steps and immediately saw the front door ajar. As he entered, he called out to both his mom and dad. Receiving no answer, he made his way through the short entrance area and looked to his right into a stepdown living room. There he saw his father lying face down, (Slide advance) his head covered with bloody matted hair. Logan, said his attention immediately focused on his father's two severed hands that had been strategically placed above his father's head.

"It's as if the hands were praying," Jeannie interrupted.

"Exactly," replied Farnsworth. "According to the medical examiner, it appears they were removed postmortem as there was little arterial spray during their removal. Logan quickly notified dispatch requesting a backup, EMTs and fire. He continued to call out to his mother, but getting no answer, he drew his weapon and headed down the hallway toward the kitchen.

"The bedrooms are all located at the back of the house. As soon as he turned into the kitchen, he saw his mother lying face up on the floor with her blouse ripped open. (Slide advance) Both breasts had been removed and placed with the nipples upright, about a foot from her side."

The next slide (Slide advance) showed a close-up of the face. Jeannie immediately noted that the eye sockets were empty; the killer had grotesquely removed the eyes. The forehead and crown also showed signs of trauma, (Slide advance) wounds that appeared similar to those of her husband.

"Within minutes that seemed like hours to Officer Logan, EMTs, Fire, and patrol backup arrived. No murder weapon was found at the scene." Lt. Farnsworth concluded and turned to Detective Dalton. "Can you and Blank take over from here?"

Jeannie watched as both Detectives Dalton and Blank stood in front of the podium instead of behind it. Both had booming voices. Jeannie thought Dalton looked like Sean Connery in his later James Bond films, but he did not have the voice.

Dalton spoke first. "We arrived at the scene thirty-four minutes after being advised of the homicides." Redirecting his gaze toward Jeannie, he continued. "Nearly everyone knew Officer Logan's parents. They were good people. They'd worked that farm all their lives, raising Halloween pumpkins, and in the fall inviting our officers to bring their kids out there for a free pumpkin, and offering all of us you-pick vegetable days in the summertime. No one spoke a bad word about them. They were a very respected family.

"Agent Loomis, most of our homicides are either drug or gang related. Some stem from arguments that escalate. Home invasions are uncommon in our rural areas. That said, the EMTs and fire units had already left before we got there. The medical examiner arrived the same time we did, but we convinced him to let us see the scene before he and the crime scene technicians entered." Glancing at Detective Blank, he asked him to take over.

Blank appeared much younger than his partner, his long blond hair falling below his collar. He was more of a dresser than Dalton. *Must be a little generational difference between the two*, Jeannie thought. Blank began, "We interviewed Officer Logan who reviewed the route he took inside the house and what he observed when he arrived. He was in shock, so after we got what we needed we had another officer take him to the station. Dalton and I entered the residence, trying to avoid the numerous blood deposits in route. The first victim we saw was the elderly Mr. Logan."

More slides were shown with Blank not really providing much more information than had already been presented. The slides showed various views of the bodies, with blood droplets splattered on the floor as well as ceiling and walls. Jeannie was particularly interested in the severed hands positioning, and Mrs. Logan's breast and eye removals. She wondered how much time it would take to remove the body parts and then position the hands in a praying-like position, and prop up the breasts as they were found? *Something to ponder*, she thought. Having been presented with this information, she knew where the media got the killer's moniker.

"There was a considerable amount of blood everywhere, but not as much as we would have expected given the mutilations. The medical examiner said it appeared that both victims were killed before the removed body parts were removed. Prints at the scene all matched the victims, relatives and friends of the family. No prints were found on the clawhammer. Autopsies showed that body parts were removed with a very sharp, non-serrated single sided blade. Research to determine the type of tool used is ongoing. The female victim's eyes were not located. The killer either disposed of them or took them with him."

Jeannie heard what was being said, but fixated on the praying hands and the breasts slide. *Why did he take the female's eyes, and not the male's? Overkill? Religion? Cult? Maybe!* she thought.

Detective Blank stopped to sip his Coke and continued. "Dalton and I walked the rest of the house, and in this bedroom used as a den (slide advance) we found several volumes of an old Encyclopedia Britannica thrown on the floor. I thumbed through several pages and found several one hundred dollar bills inserted between the pages. One book contained over one-thousand dollars and the other two totaled seven-hundred more. We then went through all of the books in the bookcase and found ten-thousand, three hundred dollars more.

"We interviewed family members who confirmed that the Logan's had twelve-thousand dollars stashed away. The killer didn't find any of their hidden money. Dalton and I feel that the killer was interrupted, and consequently missed the hidden cash. He was very close. Perhaps when Officer Logan arrived to check on his parents, he was scared off. We don't know for sure." Blank turned the presentation back over to Lt. Farnsworth. Farnworth looked a Jeannie and asked if it would be alright to continue, and handle questions later? Jeannie nodded in agreement.

Farnsworth added that when Dalton and Blank searched the perimeter of the residence, they found the phone line into the house had been cut, as well as the wires to the alarm system. "They learned that neither of the Logans had cellphones. Both thought they were too old to learn the technology. No prints were found at the junction box. They also found that one of the garage windows had been removed and placed against the house wall, concluding this was probably the point of entry. The killer appeared to have had enough time to use a knife to remove the putty around the window and take out the pane of glass.

(Slide advance) "As you can see in this slide, the window is camouflaged behind this tree and bush. No one would have seen him if they passed on the road. Patrol officers contacted all nearby neighbors, but this is a rural area where houses are spread out on an acreage--not like a typical residential area. No one noticed anything unusual. OK, let's take a short--and I mean short--five-minute break and then we'll resume."

Jeannie asked Lt. Farnsworth about backgrounds. "Yes, to date on this kill we have sixty-seven background returns, all negative. These were relatives, friends, neighbors, associates – all negative."

"Huh," Jeannie replied. "How about bank record checks?"

"They had joint accounts. Everything seems above board, like Dalton said. These were upstanding citizens, and it seems that no one had a grudge on them."

Jeannie turned to see a fairly young detective dressed in a suit waiting to talk with her. "Agent Loomis, I was in your class about three years ago at Evergreen College. You talked about serial killers and said that generally they have a type of victim they hunt. I'm Terry White, by the way."

"Hi Terry. Nice to meet you again. I recognized you when I entered, but like I said, the memory is not what it once was," she said, which was a lie. She could not place him from her junior college class. "So, you're part of the task force?" she asked.

"Yes, I'm next up," pointing to the podium. "Agent Loomis, it was a bad one."

Farnsworth taped on the podium microphone and everyone returned to their seats. Detective White stood near a side wall waiting to be called.

CHAPTER EIGHT

At 9:15 a.m., cab driver Mahmood Abass, the only eye-witness to the killing, arrived at the San Francisco FBI office to meet with Ismail Flores. Flores hoped that Abass could provide forensic artist Sheila Barnard with valuable information she could use to construct a sketch of the cop killer.

After the meeting, Sheila told Ismail that Abass had a great memory for detail and that she was very confident the drawing they came up with would be reasonably accurate. She added that Abass recalled that the suspect wore braces. Ismail gave the drawing to one of his agents, asking that it be sent to all media outlets with a request they show it on their networks. More importantly, Flores told the agent to blanket all dentists and orthodontists in the bay area to see if they recognized the sketched image as one of their patients.

The following day, a $50,000 reward was offered for information leading to the suspect's arrest. This led to hundreds of received phone calls needing followed up. By that afternoon alone, phone calls received from the public as well as dentists and orthodontists totaled over a hundred possible suspects that were passed on to Flores and his team. Ismail assigned his agents to work around-the-clock shifts.

SAC Lomax had told Ismail earlier that all resources including manpower was available, and Ismail took him up on the offer. Not one agent complained about working seven days a week. Someone had declared war on the thin blue line by stalking and killing police officers, and everyone wanted in on the hunt.

After an intensive week of whittling down phoned-in tips and eliminating subjects, Flores sensed that frustration was setting in among the team. They needed a break, and they got it Saturday night.

Officer Roy Graham enjoyed his job with the SFPD. A patrol officer for the preceding 6 years, he believed that by flying below the radar when it came to politics was the way to advance in the department. On the first of his three-day break and with the weather unseasonably warm, he took his wife and twin ten-year old daughters, Janet and Monica, to Pier 39 and a tour of Alcatraz Island. After parking their minivan in the pre-paid parking lot, he bought admission to the Wax Museum. This was a first for his daughters who were amazed at how life-like the celebrities looked. They loved being able to interact with the creations, even using some props. There was no time limit at the museum, but Roy kept checking his watch so they would be first in line for the Red and White ferry that would take them to the famous island.

Beginning to tire and getting hungry, his daughters wanted something to eat, so they left the museum and caught a quick bite at a fast food stand near a souvenir shop on the pier. Finished with their lunch, they walked over to Pier 33 and stood in line for ten minutes before boarding the ferry with others holding tickets for that boarding time. He didn't notice that a white male wearing a San Francisco Giants baseball hat had been watching him and his family from the time they parked their car to joining them on the same ferry to the island. For several weeks, Officer Graham had been stalked as he traveled from the Potrero district station house to his home.

Roy's kids loved riding on the top deck, hoping to spot either seals or dolphins. Harbor porpoises and bottlenose dolphins had found new habitats in San Francisco Bay and were now regularly seen foraging for fish and bodysurfing in boat wakes generated by ferries as they plied the bay to Alcatraz and out under the Golden Gate Bridge. It became too cool for them on deck, so the entire family went inside where Roy bought his daughters and wife hot chocolate at the ferry's café. The white male followed from a safe distance.

Earlier, Roy had tried to explain The Rock's history to his daughters, but he was not very successful. His wife reminded him they were only ten-years old. Undeterred, Roy shared facts about the famous prison to Nancy who at least led him to believe she was interested. He knew she had seen the old Clint Eastwood movie *Escape from Alcatraz* and told her it was pretty accurate. They both saw Sean Connery and Nicholas Gage in the 1996 American action thriller *The Rock*, and she remarked how cool it would be if either of the famous actors were on the island when they got there. Of course, neither of his daughters knew Connery or Gage.

The fifteen-minute boat trip seemed unbearably long to his daughters who kept asking when they would get there. Finally, the boat docked and they deboarded. The children ran ahead and up the ramp to the waiting tour guide. Roy knew the family would not be able to take in all prison sights due to his kids limited attention span, but he felt proud that they would remember this day. Nancy was particularly interested in the cells lining the cellblocks and could not imagine being confined in such a small space for years on end. "Don't do the crime, if you can't do the time," Roy said with a laugh. The white male who overheard his comment did not react.

Roy continued to give his personal tour. "That's the cell that housed the Bird Man of Alcatraz, Albert Stroud, but animals were not allowed as pets, so the name is something that followed him from his previous prison incarceration. And that cell belonged to Scarface Al Capone. He was later released since syphilis had reached his brain and his days were numbered. He later died at his mansion in Florida."

"Gee, my husband, the historian," Roy's wife commented. "How many times did you say you've been here?"

"Ismail, we have a possible suspect," Agent Parson told him when arriving at work Saturday morning. Showing Ismail a booking photo, he told him the person's name was DeShawn Roberts, a twenty-nine year old parolee. "He did three years at Folsom for carjacking before being transferred to San Quentin after he stabbed a white guard. Did seven years for the assault. His parole agent is the one who called us after seeing the photo. Said it could be him."

"Jesus! What took him so long to call?" Ismail asked.

Parson replied, "He was on a European vacation with his wife and just got back to work."

"OK. Where does this DeShawn Roberts live?" asked Ismail.

"The parolee officer, Eddie Stevens, said he could contact Roberts who's due for his monthly check-in. We could be there and do an interview with Stevens present. Stevens can assert a little pressure if Roberts tells us to fuck off. I told him I'd call him back once I ran it past you."

"OK, sounds good. Call him back and tell him to notify us as soon as a date and time have been set. Good job Parson." *Things might be starting to come together*, Ismail thought as he walked to his office. He checked in with SAC Lomax and let him know about the recent possibility, and that he and Agent Parson would interview Parsons at a later date.

The two ten-year old's were exhausted and fell asleep in the van before Roy made it back to the Bay Bridge for the drive home. Although he and his wife did not like Berkeley and what the city had become, they found a good housing deal from a friend of a friend, and were currently renting an older two-bedroom apartment there. The apartment did not come with a garage or even a carport, but he was fortunate to finding a parking space almost in front of their residence. The apartment was at least two miles from the University of California campus, so most student foot traffic did not affect their neighborhood.

Nancy carried one of the twins while Roy got the other. He headed back to the van once Nancy took over the chore of getting the girls in bed, exiting the apartment and opening the rear hatch to the van to retrieve some of the girls' clothing. The suspect approached out of the shadows and fired two rounds, one in the back of Roy's head, the second lower--severing his spine. Roy never saw him approach and died a few seconds after falling to the street.

Two neighbors heard the gun shots, and looking out of their respective windows saw a white blond haired male run to a parked motorcycle and speed out of the area, performing a wheelie in the process. Both called 9-1-1 and reported the shooting.

Ismail and Agent Parson stood in a room adjacent to that of Parole Agent Stevens. They did not want DeShawn Roberts to run if he spotted them; he was to think the meeting was a required, routine parole check-in. Five-minutes later, Agent Stevens called Flore's, informing him that Roberts had just shown up and that he would be escorting Roberts back to his office. As planned, they waited until they heard Stevens start a conversation with Roberts before walking into his office. Roberts looked up at both Flores and Parson, but did not show any sign of distress or nervousness. Flores made their identity known to Roberts as Parson displayed his badge. Again, there was no sign of panic.

"You are DeShawn Roberts, is that correct?" Flores asked.

"What's it to you? And why's the FBI questioning me?" he asked, the latter half of the statement drawn out in a partial slur. He glancing back at Stevens.

Stevens spoke before Flores could respond. "First, DeShawn, I expect your cooperation with Agents Flores and Parson. They're here following up on a serious matter, and they hope you might be able to shed some light on a case."

"Mr. Roberts, where were you on the night and early morning of April 22nd and early morning of April 23th?" Ismail asked.

"What's this all about? You trying to frame me for something I didn't do? You pigs are all alike, ain't you? How the fuck am I'm supposed to remember where I was on those dates? This is fucked up man."

Both Ismail and Parson accepted DeShawn's answer and doubted he was the shooter. Most guilty individuals have an elaborate response to the question Ismail asked. Since a guilty party would know the circumstances surrounding a crime, they usually cover for both the time before and after a criminal event. Most innocent people answer the question as DeShawn did. They have to methodically search their memory to deduce where they were on the date and time being questioned.

"Let me rephrase the question, DeShawn. Do you know where Berkley's Donuts and Mud place is?"

"Wow, wow, wow man! You all trying to get me for the cop that got wasted there? Fuck that. I'm out of here!"

"Sit down!" Steven yelled at Roberts. "You'll leave when I tell you to leave. Now, I suggest you answer Agent Flore's questions, or I'll wrap your ass up on a parole violation and you can spend a few days in county lockup."

Flores could see the rage and hatred in Roberts' demeanor, but it was not what he would expect if Roberts were a cop killer. "Want to try to answer my question again, or do you need me to repeat it?"

"I remember your question Mr. FBI. I know where that donut shop is, but I've never gone there. If you have someone who says I shot that pig, they're fucking lying. Probably some fuckin honky who wants to frame a nigger. Here's a surprise for you, and you too Stevens. I want to take a lie detector test, right here, right now. Yeah, you get me strapped into a lie detector right now and I'll show you that I didn't go into no donut shop and shoot a cop. Then, once I pass, I'm going to sue your asses, that's what I'm going to do."

After this drama, Flores eliminated Roberts as the suspect, primarily because the shooter did not go into the donut shop--he shot officer Grayson from outside.

"I have one other question Mr. Roberts, and then if it's OK with Agent Stevens, you can go."

"What other question?" Roberts grumbled.

"Do you know the bar near the SFPD headquarters?"

"Yeah, I know it. So what?" Roberts glared at both Flores and Parson, thinking they were trying to trick him.

"Have you ever gone there?" Flores asked.

"Are you fucking crazy man? Why in the hell would a black man want to get a drink inside that pig's bar?" Roberts replied, laughing and slouching lower in his chair.

"Sorry. One final question. Do you have a gun?"

"This is harassment! You know damn well that if I get caught with a weapon, it's back to the joint.

Do I have a gun? Fuck no! Can I go now?" he asked, looking at Stevens.

Stevens looked at Flores and could see from his expression that Roberts should be allowed to leave. "Yes, DeShawn, you can leave and thank you for your cooperation."

"I'm fuckin out of here. You're all going to hear from my attorney," Roberts said as he forcibly pushed his chair back to make a statement.

"There went our most promising lead to date," Parson's said as he and Flores walked down the parole office hallway to the exit. "Our only lead to date," Flores responded. "Back to square one."

CHAPTER NINE

The next morning, Flore's wife interrupted him while he was shaving. "Izzy, your cellphone started ringing in the other room. Here it is," she said, placing buzzing phone next to the basin.

"Thanks Babe," he said as he wiped shaving crème from the side of his face and grabbed the phone. "Hello, sorry it took so long to answer. I was shaving." It was the SAC.

"Flores. This may or may not be related to your investigation, but an off-duty SFPD officer was killed yesterday afternoon while you were interviewing that parolee. He was ambushed outside his home. Witnesses said the suspect was Caucasian. Again, maybe it's not related."

"Or, we might have a salt and pepper team of cop killers on our hands," Flores conjectured. "I'll be leaving shortly. Can you transfer me to Stephanie?"

Occasionally, Stephanie filled in for Jeannie when her normal receptionist was off duty. Ismail liked to think of Stephanie as his receptionist, which she seemed to not only accept, but liked. "Hello Ismail. What do you need?" she asked in a cheery voice.

"Hi, Stephanie. I'm getting ready to leave the house, heading to the SFPD. The SAC told me they had one of their own killed last night in an ambush, and I want to get what they have so far. Contact Darcy, Burk and Parson, as well as the rest of the team, and have them in the briefing room by noon today to review everything we have, plus whatever I glean from the SFPD."

Two hours later, Ismail returned to the bureau. After checking in with Stephanie and grabbing a cup of coffee, he headed to the larger of the two briefing rooms. SAC Lomax was already present with the rest of the team. With no time to waste, Ismail quickly filled his team in with what he had learned at the SFPD.

"Officer Roy Graham, six-year vet with the PD, lived with his family, wife and two kids in Berkeley, down from the main campus. After he and his wife got his two girls to bed, he returned to their van to gather up their belonging from a long day at Pier 39 and Alcatraz. As he reached into the van, the assailant approached from the rear and shot him twice.

"Two witnesses who heard the shots and quickly looked out their respective windows saw a Caucasian male jump on a motorcycle and tear out of there. Both witnesses are positive the suspect was a white male. So, ladies and gentlemen, it appears we have a team of cop killers on our hands, not just one."

Reaching for another pizza slice, Justin laughed at Jerome. "After my hit yesterday afternoon, I guess we're even, huh? That officer never knew what hit him. I mean, when he hit the ground his body didn't even twitch."

"Yeah, not bad for a white boy," Jerome said, grabbing another slice of pizza. "Took you long enough to tie me, asshole--doing all that surveillance and shit before you put him down. That's not for me. Find them and shoot them, I say."

"Hey, but that's part of the fun--lets me do a little James Bonding and experience the thrill of the hunt, nigger. You should try it sometime," Justin retorted.

"You got to be kidding me. I'm going to follow some pig around for a few days before putting some lead in him, or her for that matter. In fact, I think the next dead cop will be a cunt. How about that, you jive-ass turkey? Tomorrow I strike again, you'll see."

Detective Terry White approached the podium after being introduced by Lt. Farnsworth. White nodded at the computer technician who showed a slide of an old farm-style home in much better shape than those of previous victims.

"This is Mr. and Mrs. James Shanahan's house. The couple lived at this address for 52 years, a spread that covers 80 acres, mostly in walnuts and almonds." The following slide showed a photo of the elderly couple taken in front of their house and surrounded by what Jeannie surmised were their children and grandchildren.

"On June fifteenth, Raul Mendoza and his brother, Saul Mendoza, arrived at the farm to do orchard maintenance. They normally check in at the main house to let either of the Shanahan's know they are there so they can get paid later in the week. Raul knocked on the door several times, but got no answer. Thinking they should be home and feeling it strange they were not getting a response, Saul went to this side (pointing) of the covered porch and peeked in the windows to see if there were any activity inside—or if the Shanahans simply hadn't heard the knocking (Slide advance).

"This window (pointing again) looks into the master bedroom. Saul jumped back and shouted upon peering in. Raul quickly joined him. Through the window saw both Shanahans lying face-up on their bed covered in blood. The men ran to Raul's truck where he'd left his cellphone and called 9-1-1." Detective White nodded in the area of the projector and another slide appeared.

"Officers Child and Nunes, a two-man unit, arrived at the scene and met up with the Mendoza brothers who shared what they'd seen. Leaving the men at their truck, the two officers climbed onto the porch and found the front door locked. They peered into the bedroom window and saw the two bloody victims. Nunes went around the house and found the backdoor also locked. Hearing that the backdoor was also locked, Child's splintered the door frame with a hard kick and gained entrance. During their brief cursory search looking for suspects and other victims, they noted that neither the kitchen nor living room seemed disturbed, nor the sole bathroom and guest bedroom. The master bedroom was a different matter."

Jeannie noticed that Detective White did not have to refer to notes as he described the grisly findings at the Shanahan's residence. She knew from experience that this case would follow him to his grave, just like the many situations she had confronted during her law enforcement career.

Just like combat veterans, the brain tries to shield itself from ongoing memories of violence; but at times, they return with almost the same intensity experienced during the original event. She remembered something a pathologist told her during an autopsy. He said that most cops thrive in spite of the stress they encounter daily during their careers; but for some reason, once they retire and the stress is removed, they are more likely to suffer a massive heart attack. She forced herself to focus on White's continuing presentation.

He again nodded in the area of the projectionist and a bloody scene filled the screen. Both Shanahan bodies were marked by ghastly penetrations to the head. It reminded Jeannie of being a kid and smashing Halloween pumpkins with a hammer after the holiday, before tossing them in the garbage can.

Mr. Shanahan appeared to be the most mutilated. His head and face seemed to have imploded. Jeannie then noticed that Mrs. Shanahan's body had most of the head hair removed and laying by her side, matted with blood. Her eyes looked strange. She would later find out why.

"As you can see, both victims received numerous head traumas. Autopsies showed that Mrs. Shanahan received seven blows to her head, and Mr. Shanahan received eleven." White stopped his narrative while looking at the photo on the screen. Jeannie thought that perhaps he was trying to suppress his feelings (Slide advance).

"The officers studied the bodies more closely and saw that Mr. Shanahan's penis and eyes had been removed, and both of Mrs. Shanahan breasts were missing. Additionally, they noted that she had been scalped and her hair was left along the left side of her body near the side of the bed. Her eyes had also been removed from their sockets. My partner and I arrived at the site thirty-seven minutes later and took over the scene."

"Excuse me, Detective White. Were any of the missing body parts found in the bedroom or the rest of the house?" Jeannie asked.

Without answering, White nodded again at the projectionist and another photo appeared, showing a frying pan on top of the stove in the kitchen. Inside the pan were two breasts faced upward with the penis at the base, creating a sadistic Happy Face smile. In a second pan were Mrs. Shanahan's eyes. "This is where we found the body parts. The coroner doesn't think anything had been fried or eaten."

Sick fuck! Jeannie thought.

Another slide appeared, showing a wooden framed window where the putty had been removed. "We determined this to be the point of entry," White said. Silence filled the room. Jeannie thought that everyone's thoughts, including hers, were on the "frying pans" slide.

White continued, "We found a safe opened in the master bedroom closet. In checking with the Shanahan's children, they said their parents kept over $100,000 in cash there in case the economy went south."

"Alright everyone. Let's take another short break," Lt. Farnsworth said, and walking over to Jeannie commented, "I hate to say I told you so."

"You're right," Jeannie responded. "This guy seems to do more planning than the Night Stalker. He takes advantage of a situation and spends time studying his victims' habits. So far, I believe this sicko selects his victims, studies them, picks a window for his P.O.E. (point of entry) and waits for them to fall asleep. How many kills can you attribute to him?"

As officers returned to their seats and Farnworth began to stand, he whispered to Jeannie, "Five separate incidents, with eleven dead."

Killings three and four appeared to be carbon copies of the first two. Elderly victims were rousted from their beds or killed in them. They all had been brutally assaulted with an object and then post-mortem dissected. The male victims had either their hands, feet, or penis removed. The females had their hair, breasts, and eyes removed, but did not violate their vaginal area.

Starting with what the SJPD believed to be his second kill, the Shanahan's, the murderer placed removed body parts on the stove in a frying pan. In kill number four, he appeared to have eaten some of the parts, and in kill number five he cooked consumed parts of each item removed from the deceased. His bizarre behavior was escalating, Jeannie thought, and that was not a good sign.

The final presentation was made by Sergeant Lucy Gibson. She appeared to be in her early forties and was slightly overweight for her height. Her hair was cut in a masculine style, and judging by her speaking manner, Jeannie assumed she was a lesbian. Gibson talked through a series of slides in what might be described as a booming voice. What she presented suggested behavioral patterns similar to those of other killings, with one exception.

"This is little eight-year old Janie Potter, the granddaughter of the victims," Gibson began. The slide showed a small girl lying on a bed in pink Minnie Mouse pajamas. "There was no sign of blood or evidence of blunt force trauma, but a closeup photo of her throat showed signs of strangulation. The killer had placed the hands of the body together as if it were praying. In the kitchen we found this on the table." (Slide advance) Jeannie saw a large dinner plate with a fork lying across the top. In the center was half an eyeball and one breast. The killer was now enjoying his desire for cannibalism. Jeannie felt bile entering her throat, but swallowed to stop its travel upward. "We suspect that young Janie was visiting her grandparents and was at the wrong place at the wrong time."

The only new piece of information Jeannie learned during the presentations was that the coroner had ruled out a common clawhammer as the murder weapon. Jeannie made a mental note: *weapon identification needed.*

Late afternoon arrived before all presentations were completed. Lt. Farnsworth dismissed everyone and told them to reconvene the next morning so that Jeannie could have time to process what she had just learned. It was almost 4 p.m., and Jeannie felt that if she hurried, she might beat the commuter traffic and make it back to her house in Newark. That thought was a miscalculation. It still took her almost one and a half hours to make the short twenty-mile drive. So much for the old days when she could even make it over the mountain and down into Santa Cruz in an hour.

CHAPTER TEN

As Ismail was checking-in the next morning, Stephanie told him that over 1,000 phone calls had come in following the last media showing of the artist's sketch. "Anything back from dentists or orthodontists?" he asked. "Nothing yet, but we can hope," she answered.

"Yeah, but in the meantime this son-of-a bitch could be stalking another officer," Ismail fired back--and then apologized to Stephanie for his brusque remark.

"It's OK. Everyone's exhausted," came the reply. "Something has to break soon."

By the end of the week, hundreds of possible suspects had been eliminated one by one. Ismail was starting to feel the pressure as the task force leader. Thousands of manpower hours were being spent and the team was no closer to catching the two cop killers.

The following Wednesday evening, Officer Sharon Little was sitting in her patrol car outside a liquor store on San Francisco's Van Ness Ave. Crime was up in all parts of the city, especially in this area, so the liquor store owners negotiated with the SFPD and paid for a uniformed officer to be present during the nighttime hours. A single mother of a 7-year-old boy, Officer Little needed the extra money to pay for babysitting and other unexpected expenses.

It was not hard for her to stay awake most nights, but her little boy had an ear infection the night before and she was operating on little sleep. She turned the patrol car radio up to a loud level and closed her eyes, figuring that anything hot being broadcast would wake her up. She never sensed the masked gunman approaching her vehicle on the driver's side. At close range he fired nine rounds through the window into her body. She never had a chance. He then reached into the vehicle, stole her service .45 Glock, and walked away.

A male standing at a nearby corner witnessed the whole thing. He ran across the street to the patrol car and saw Officer Little sloped over on her side, held in place by her seatbelt. He quickly pulled out his cellphone and called 9-1-1, describing what he had seen and the direction he saw the gunman flee.

SFPD patrol units arrived and conducted a preliminary interview of the witness. He told them the gunman simply appeared out of the darkness and walked toward the driver's side of the patrol car. The officer never looked up. "When he was a foot away from the window, he raised his hand and then, boom, boom, boom, over and over again. It was like he had a machine gun. Then he reached through the broken driver's window and I saw him take her gun. He put it in his waistband over his stomach, turned and walked away. That poor lady officer, she didn't see him coming. Oh Lordy."

When detectives arrived at the scene, it did not take long for everyone to reach the same conclusion. There was no apparent motive, no warning, just an execution of another officer. The pattern seemed to match the other cop shootings. SAC Lomax was notified and he, in turn, notified Ismail Flores who sent Agent Parson to the scene to gather information that would be needed later and shared with his team.

"It has to be a salt and pepper team," Ismail said to SAC Lomax. "It's like they're in competition. If the donut shop shooting was the first one, they've been playing this game now for five months."

CHAPTER ELEVEN

Jeannie's tedious drive home from the San Jose Police Department was finally over. "That was a hell-of-a-commute," she said to her seven koi fish swimming around in the 500-gallon aquarium. She initially purchased the aquarium as a room divider shortly after her fiancé, Ricky Pinheiro, died in a shootout with an urban terrorist group in Concord. Thinking the sound of the filter and bubbles might be form of meditation to help her get over her loss, she placed it in her large formal dining room where she sometimes sat and ate dinner. Most of the time, she ate sitting on the couch watching television, or if it she had food described as a "wet sandwich," she ate it standing over the sink in the kitchen like her dad had done when she still lived at home.

Her late father and her uncle occasionally built koi ponds for clients interested in a having a backyard Japanese garden, so she was familiar with koi varieties. It seemed that every house she lived in with her parents before leaving the nest had a koi pond. Koi were generally expensive, as were hers.

She had two Kohokus (red and white), a Tancho (white body with a red circle on the crown), an Utsurimono (black and white spots), a Taisho Sanshoku (red, white, and black spots), a yellow and black Hi Utsuri, and her favorite--a Shusui, having a red and white head, red and pale blue sides, with dark spots running down its spine. She did not go so far as to give each fish a name; she talked to all of them in general. None of them responded to her commute from hell comment that evening.

The koi swam to the surface, expecting to be fed, and they were not disappointed as Jeannie dropped several food pellets into their water world. They quickly grabbed a food pellet and then dove part way into the depth of the tank, only to quickly resurface and grab another. "You guys eat like Ismail," she said out loud. Right on cue, her cellphone rang. It was Ismail. "Hey Ace, how's your investigation going?" she asked without saying hello.

"Well, since you asked—it's extremely shitty. We now know it's a salt and pepper team doing the shootings, but so far there's not a Goddamned lead. I think these two are in competition, always trying to outdo the other. We thought an ex-con might be good for it. You know, the pepper half of the team, but that didn't pan out. We need a damned break. And I can tell you, I think the SAC's starting to feel some heat, but there's nothing I can think of that we haven't looked at or focused on. How about you and your serial?"

Jeannie looked down at her dining table and saw that she had already opened her briefcase and removed pictures and documents she would soon add to the display on her second upstairs bedroom wall. She had all of the autopsy reports she needed to review the case. There was something about the wounds that told her she needed to focus on those.

"This is one sick puppy, Flo. The media calls him the mutilator, but they don't know the half of it. He's morphed into cannibalism. Like you, we need some small little break that will help us re-focus our investigation. About Lomax--don't worry about him. He can take whatever heat comes his way, but always make sure you keep him in the loop."

Jeannie's doorbell rang. Quickly wishing Flores good luck on his investigation and hanging up, she grabbed her gun and walked to the front door. Looking through the peephole, she saw the last person she wanted to see that night. Standing in her normal hair curlers was none other than her pesky, nosey, gossipy next door neighbor, Delores.

"Hello Delores," she said opening the front door.

"Hi Jeannie, I'm so sorry to intrude on you, but I felt I needed to confess about something I did today while feeding your fish."

"Well, since I had seven fish when I left, and seven when I counted a little while ago, you apparently didn't kill any," Jeannie said with a smile.

"Oh, God no! I would never kill one of God's little creatures. No, instead I sadly violated your privacy, but I didn't mean too. You see, when I came in at noon to feed the koi, I noticed you left your upstairs bedroom light on." She pointed to the second bedroom and continued her story. "Well, when I got up there, I couldn't help but notice those dreadful pictures hanging on the wall. I almost gagged and had to sit in your desk chair because I felt faint. My God, all that blood. I don't know how you do it Jeannie."

Jeannie had not removed the photos of her last serial investigation involving Daniel Koufax. He murdered numerous females in and around Marin county, leaving several of their bodies in motel bathtubs. Fortunately, she had not replaced them with the more gruesome photos of the recent mutilation cases.

"First, Delores, no need to apologize, and thank you for turning off the light. My PG&E electrical bill is high enough without extra lights being left on. I'm sorry you had to see those terrible pictures. I put them on my wall and study them for possible inspiration when trying to solve a case. Sometimes while doing this I see something I originally missed, and that leads to solving the case--similar to when you helped me solve that serial killer case with Koufax. In fact, the photos you saw related to that case. That one was frustrating since it was never what we cops call a who-done-it case."

Jeannie could have further explained to Delores that in the Koufax case, the killer left plenty of forensic evidence behind. Besides semen, fingerprints, and signed motel registration forms in which he used his own name, he was captured on parking lot surveillance cameras driving away in victim's vehicles after he killed them. Jeannie said he was playing a *Time Game*, always one step--or a few minutes--ahead of responding officers.

"Delores, some innocent information you provided solved that case." Jeannie remembered how her neighbor did, in fact, help solve the serial killer case. On an occasion when Jeannie was trying to escape the neighborhood without running into Delores, she was unlucky. However, it was actually a blessing in disguise. Delores and husband Walter told her about a movie they had watched on HBO called "The Highwaymen." It was a 2019 film starring Kevin Costner and Woody Harrelson. The lead characters came out of Texas Rangers retirement at the request of the governor played by Kathy Bates, and their task was to track down the Bonny and Clyde gang who were terrorizing the southern United States. No matter how hard the two Rangers searched for Bonny and Clyde, they were always too late. Finally, it dawned on the two aging lawmen that the lawless pair always returned to their familiar haunts when the heat was turned up on their gang. Friends and relatives provided them with safe shelter.

That stirred Jeannie's creative juices. She thanked Delores and Walter, drove as fast as she could across the Dumbarton bridge, and headed directly to the bureau with a successful plan that caught Koufax. Jeannie later credited Delores in neighborhood talk, along with delivering an expensive bottle of champagne to her and her husband.

Complimenting Delores for her help in solving the Koufax case hit home again. "Well, I just wanted to help," Delores said, touching her curlers. "What case are you working on now? Maybe I can help."

What the hell, Jeannie thought. Maybe her dingbat neighbor might provide some insight again. "This has to stay confidential Delores. You understand, don't you?"

"Of course, Jeannie. You can trust me." Jeannie gave a short synopsis of the case, explaining that all kills occurred in old farm houses on large acreages. She left out the mutilation part. "You know, those houses you describe remind me of places my cousins used to live in, both in Modesto and Turlock." Before Jeannie could interject anything, Delores continued. "My auntie and uncle had 10 acres of apricots in the foothills above Mission Boulevard in Hayward. Each summer my mom and dad would take me and my two brothers there to pick apricots so my mom could can them." Delores began to laugh as she continued. "We had to use these three-legged ladders you pressed against a tree and then climbed, carrying a bucket. God, I can't believe no one fell. At first I ate more than I put in my bucket." She finally took a pause, but then continued. "It was so much fun, although sometimes I barely made it home without having an accident, if you know what I mean. Apricots just seem to go right through me. Sometimes it was scary though. You see, with so many trees and fruit to be picked, my auntie and uncle had to hire a bunch of Mexicans to come in and harvest the fruit before it got ruined or eaten by the damned birds. Some of those workers would just stare at me. I was too young to realize what they were probably thinking. It's like those illegals you see in the morning hanging around Home Depot and Lowe's looking for work. The contractors you know, they pay them under the table. No names, no record of their employment. All illegal. Gee, look who I'm talking to about something illegal. Sorry."

"Delores! My God, you may have done it again! I need to excuse myself so I can make a few phone calls. Thank you so much! Oh, and thank you for taking care of my fish." Delores, turning and seeing the front door closing, continued, "What, what did I say?" Jeannie had no time to reply.

Delores started a slow walk back to her house, quizzing herself over what she had just said. "How about that. I helped solved another FBI case," she said to herself. Stopping once to pick up a curler that fell from her head, she could hardly wait to get in the house and tell Walter the news.

CHAPTER TWELVE

Instead of making phone calls, Jeannie grabbed a diet Dr. Pepper from the refrigerator and headed upstairs, saying goodnight to the koi and turning off their overhead lamp on the way. "Sorry guys, I need to get some work done. Sleep tight."

She spread the autopsy documents and photos she brought home out on her desk. The autopsy notes were meticulous. Each separate autopsy report was eight pages in length and included two outside wound sketches in actual size, and a human skull profile showing penetration locations and shapes.

"Weird. These entrance wounds look like a triangle. An isosceles triangle, if I remember my geometry," she said out loud to herself. The outside wound was roughly circular in shape, slightly larger than a quarter. She began reading the coroner's statement for each autopsy.

It stated that the blow caused a penetrating wound that fractured the right occipital bone, and pierced the right occipital lobe. This caused hemorrhaging and resulting rupture into the posterior fossa and forth ventricle, causing acute compression of the brain stem and subsequent death."

"Starting to get too technical, doctor," Jeannie again said to herself. "Note to self. I need to sit down and talk with him, especially about the wounds." Before reviewing the other crime scenes photos, she took a hot bubble bath, thinking about what Delores had said about extra workers needed to tend the crops. *Another possibility. Could the suspect be a part-time farm helper?* she thought.

It was right there in front of us all the time, she thought. *Damn Delores, you're good.* Looking up to heaven she said, "Hey Ricky, Delores may have solved another one." She caught a tear running from her left eye and wiped it away.

While in the bathtub surrounded by lavender bubbles, she tried to switch her thoughts to another subject and clear her mind, hoping that when she got into her second bedroom she would be creatively inspired again. The approach did not work. Her thoughts continued to revolve around what Delores said. She got out of the tub and semi-dried herself, the excess moisture on her skin making it difficult to easily pull up her pajama bottoms and pull down her Thin Blue Line t-shirt. Finally dressed, she made her way to the second bedroom.

Jeannie turned on the desk lamp and the two spot lamps hanging from the upper edge of her whiteboard, illuminating documents and various gruesome photos taken at the killing sites. Picking up her black dry-marker and moving to the far left of the board, she began writing random thoughts; some of which she would use the following day when she gave her P.D. presentation.

#1. Killer knew victims, thus had to eliminate them
#2. Killer knew layout of the residence
#3. Killer came armed with weapon
#4. Killer knew something of value was in each residence
#5. Killer knew he had time
#6. Killer knows about forensic evidence
#7. Intervals between kills are shortening
#8. Killer now into cannibalism
#9. Possibly more than one killer
#10. Victims hired killer as extra help

Areas to explore:
#1. Murder weapon identification
#2. Origin of extra help during picking season (Thank you, Delores)

CHAPTER THIRTEEN

Jeannie had a restless night, thinking of the intervals between homicides. If the killer kept to his current timetable, he would strike again in the next few days. Giving up on sleep and making a cup of coffee at 3:15 a.m., she went to her second bedroom and started making notes on what she wanted to say to her task force in a few hours. She also did a quick search on her laptop, trying to find a phone number for the University of California, Berkeley's History Department, and more specifically, the Department of Hoplology--the study of weapons. Not finding it, she felt it might fall under the history domain. She hoped to find someone who could direct her to a person knowledgeable about ancient weapons, handheld axes, and hammers. Finding a likely number, she wrote it down and would call it before her San Jose commute.

Jeannie made notes about victims' head wound shapes, and selected meaningful photos taken during autopsies to share with a weapons expert, if she could find one. The pathologist who performed the various autopsies could not determine the exact type of instrument used in the killing. She got the pathologist's office number from Lt. Farnsworth's secretary and would call at 7:30 a.m., thinking that if the tool used were unique enough, it could be linked to the killer. She circled that action item on her list.

"Hello, Dr. Maitland. My name is Jeannie Loomis, and I'm with the FBI assisting the SJPD in the recent mutilation cases. Do you have a few minutes to answers some questions that have come up?"

"Agent Loomis, give me your cellphone number, and I'll call you right back," he replied. Jeannie gave it to him, and he hung up. *Guess he wants to check to see if I am who I say I am,* she thought as she waited for his return call. The call came about two minutes later.

"Sorry, but in this lentiginous culture, I needed to verify your identification. No offense."

"None taken, Doctor. I wanted to ask you about the victims' wounds."

"I already told Lt. Farnsworth and the other homicide investigators that neither I or the other pathologists here were able to determine the type of instrument used in the killings, other than their ability to inflict massive trauma to the head. I can tell you that the suspect was very strong and generated a lot of power when he struck."

"Can you give me more about his probable strength? This could aid us in identifying the suspect," she asked.

"Well, Agent Loomis. The human skull and brain are tougher than what most people believe. Hollywood has a lot to do with pushing that erroneous narrative. My colleagues and I laugh when we watch a movie and a person is shot in the head and dies instantly. That's practically impossible. I once had a suicide where the victim shot himself in the head five times before he died. Of course, he was using low velocity .22 rounds, but most of his shots bounced off his skull and embedded themselves in his bedroom ceiling. However, I've also seen rare cases where a person shoots himself on one side of the head and the bullet passes right through, exiting the opposite side."

"I understand Doctor, but about the victims we have in this case."

"I'm sorry, I digressed. Granted, there was no firearm used in your murders. My point being that the assailant had to raise his weapon a considerable height to generate the velocity needed to puncture the crowns and sides of the victims' heads. In two of the male victims, the suspect made the head entry by hitting from behind, low on the crown--meaning they were sleeping almost face down, deep into the pillow. The force of the blows allowed the weapon to pierce halfway to where the spine joins the skull. This caused death almost instantaneously."

"Do you think the suspect had medical knowledge?" Jeannie asked.

"God, no. Well, let me clarify. To hit that spot exactly, a person would need surgical experience and the victim would have to be on an operating table. No killer swinging whatever instrument could hope to hit it. No, it was just luck… I'm referring to the suspect's luck, not the poor victims."

Jeannie thought to herself that Dr. Maitland was one of those individuals who writes in a scholarly and formal style, but during normal conversation come across as an average individual not overly impressed with his own academic success.

"So, you believe death was instantaneous?" Jeannie asked.

"Close to it. If not instantaneous, it occurred within a few seconds. By the way, it appears that he used a large hunting knife for his dissections."

"Dr. Maitland, you said in your reports that the wounds were circular. Was they completely circular wounds?" Jeannie asked. She wanted to accurately describe the entrance wounds to the weapons expert, if she could find one.

"In my report, Agent, I stated the wounds appeared to be circular penetrations, and I stress the word, appeared. My colleagues and I feel they could have been triangular or even square. You see, striking the human brain is not like driving a huge nail into a block of modeling clay. Instead, when whatever tool is pulled back out of the skull, brain matter presses into the cavity. I mean, we find bone fragments, hair, blood--you name it. During the autopsies I also got the impression from the wound penetrations that the weapon you should be looking for is curved--curved downward."

"Curved?" Jeannie asked with increased curiosity.

"Yes. And afterward, the suspect had to bend forward over the victims and forcible twist and turn the weapon to remove it before delivering subsequent blows. If the spike were triangular or square, the twisting would result in a roughly circular shape."

"We think the murder weapon might have special meaning to the killer," Jeannie said, later wondering why she had made the comment.

"Why is that, if you don't mind me asking?"

"Well Doctor, in my experience, killers using bats, clubs, pipes or even a garden variety hammer wear gloves to prevent fingerprints, and then they leave their instruments of death behind at the crime scene, but not with this guy. No, this weapon means something to him. Finally, Dr. Maitland, is there anything else you can add that you didn't feel comfortable including in your report?"

"Only that this guy has a lot of anger issues that he's taking out on his victims. I'm not a law enforcement officer, but I think if you find the source of that anger, you'll go a long way in finding the suspect."

Jeannie had already decided before arriving at the SJPD that she would begin her presentation by sharing the ten insights she had the night before about the killer. She had one additional thought. There was an outside chance they were dealing with more than one killer, and that realization seemed to cover all bases.

Jeannie felt that before the team receiving assignments, they needed a more in-depth psychological profile than the one provided by Quantico. Glancing at her watch, she realized it was after 11:00 a.m. on the east coast. She picked up the phone, searched her contacts and placed the call.

CHAPTER FOURTEEN

"Jeannie Loomis. My God! How many years has it been?" exclaimed Dr. Bryan Washington, noted psychologist and professor. He had been Jeannie's dissertation advisor and teacher. Their relationship had grown from graduate student, to confidant and friend.

"Hello Doctor Washington. How are you?" Jeannie asked with a smile on her face. "I think it's been almost 15 years, maybe more. I'd have to find my bound dissertation and see what date it shows, to be precise. I'm flattered that you remember me."

"How could I not? The brightest and most inquisitive graduate student I've had in my entire 60-year career. In fact, if I recall correctly, your dissertation didn't need revision and was accepted on your first submission. Your oral defense was glowingly mentioned for several months, if I recall."

"That was only because I had a great mentor and dissertation advisor," Jeannie humbly replied.

"Now I'm the one flattered. I've followed your career with the FBI Jeannie, and I must say, I'm very proud of your accomplishments. I confess to gloating when I bring up your name with other retired professors. I remember telling you that I was a little disappointed you didn't enter the halls of academia instead of the bureau, but I'm glad I was wrong. What you've accomplished in law enforcement is breathtaking. But, I assume from this wonderful phone call at this ungodly hour on the west coast, you need to ask something. Am I correct?"

"Yes, and I do apologize for calling you so early--even in your time zone," Jeannie admitted.

"Not a problem. When you're as old as I am, you want to get up as early as possible since you don't know how many more days you have left. Fire away."

"Dr. Washington, I'm running a serial task force for the San Jose Police Department."

"Is it the mutilator case that's all over the news?" he asked.

"Yes. He's struck five times that we know of, with eleven victims so far."

"How do you know the killer is male?" the professor asked.

"I don't feel that a female would be able to take on two adults or more during the attacks, let alone remove glazing putty and remove window glass from their frames. It could be a female, but statistically and given the circumstance, my gut doesn't feel it."

"Remember what I taught you. Always rely on your gut feelings. Sorry, I interrupted you. Please go on."

"In what we believe was his first attack, he used the in-place landscaping to conceal himself while removing a window to gain entrance. All of the kill sites were farmhouses over a hundred years old set on large parcels of land used as orchards or farms. He appears to have known the victims and a home's layout. The motive appears to be greed, but the manner of his kills appears ritualistic, and it's escalating."

"In what matter is he killing?" the professor asked.

"After he gains entrance to a victim's residence, he generally waits for them to fall asleep." She explained. "Then he surprises them by hitting them in the head with a weapon that so far we've not been able to identify. Now, here's why I called you. In his first kill he cut off an elderly male victim's hands. By the way, all of his victims were elderly except a young 8-year-old girl whom we believe was at the wrong place at the wrong time. Both of the female victim's breasts had been removed and placed at her side, and both eyes had been removed.

"In his second kill, he scalped the female and left her hair by her side, and as before, removed the eyes. He removed the penis of the male as well as both hands. Those body parts were found in a frying pan in the kitchen, but had not been cooked. By his fifth kill, he morphed into full-blown cannibalism. He cooked and had eaten body parts. His time frame is now up to eleven days between kills, so he's due to commit another."

The professor remained silent as Jeannie recited the particulars of each killing. At one point she thought that perhaps she had lost the phone signal. "I'm here Jeannie. I'm trying to process everything," he said.

"I think what you're dealing with is an individual with a paraphilias called erotophonophilia. It's the most heinous of all paraphilias. Erotophonophiles have extremely violent fantasies and typically kill their victims during sex and/or mutilate their victims' sexual organs--the latter of which is usually post-mortem. Most erotophonophiles are males; there have been a few females with paraphilia, but it is rare occurrence. You said he'd been removing the male appendage, but besides female breasts, scalping, and eye removal, have any of the female sex organs been disturbed?"

"No, and there's no indication of sexual trauma either," Jeannie replied.

"Well, as you know, it's rare that an individual displays all elements of a pathology. Lust murderers are known to be psychologically and behaviorally different from those who kill out of revenge or anger displacement. Erotophonophiles typically choose their victims on the basis of sexual attractiveness, although there might be one particular physical attribute that is sexualized by a killer such as a particular body shape, hair style, and skin color. This is referred to as an erotophonophile's ideal victim type, or IVT for short. After a victim has been selected and prior to the killing, the erotophonophile may engage in a range of predatory behaviors like stalking. Perhaps this is when he scouts out the victim's houses and looks for a point of entry.

"Without getting too scholarly," he said laughing, "there was a paper that I believe was published in 1990 by Dr. P.E. Dietz and colleagues in the Bulletin of the American Academy of Psychiatry and the Law. They examined thirty sexual sadists, most of whom were sexual murderers. They found that the majority were employed white males, many married, who had a history of homosexual experiences and cross-dressing. They also reported that they had parents who had divorced or had marital infidelities, had suffered physical and/or sexual abuse, and abused drugs other than alcohol. Almost all in the sample had planned their offences and most victims were unknown to them. Some had specific targets and were motivated by greed. The victims were typically abducted or held against their will for over 24 hours, blindfolded, bound and gagged. Your killer appears to know that since the homes are secluded, hitting the victims over the head would suffice.

"Most victims were tortured. Typical abuses included forced oral sex, rape, forced insertion of foreign objects vaginally, or sex organ mutilation. Many subsequent studies have reported similar findings. However, the main problem with many of these studies is that there were no non-sadistic control groups against which the results could be compared.

"Your own department, the FBI, conducted studies and have reported that sexually sadistic murderers exhibit psychopathy and narcissism. However, other more recent studies have not found relationships with psychopathy, so it's been suggested that FBI samples may represent a particularly extreme group of sadistic sex murderers compared to other published studies. Sorry, old age has made me an old chatterbox, I'm afraid."

"Not at all," Jennie said. "Please go on."

"Another researcher compared twenty-one men who'd murdered women during sexual attacks with a hundred and twenty-one rapists who didn't kill their victims, and found that sexual murderers had significantly higher rates of social isolation and difficulties within sexual relationships. However, sexual murderers and rapists didn't differ in their utilization of pornography and deviant sexual fantasies.

"If you'd like, I can send you a couple of book chapters on sexually sadistic murderers by J. Proulx, E. Blais, and E. Beauregard. They found that sadistic sexual offenders are more likely than non-sadistic sexual offenders to have planned the kidnapping of their victims, used bondage and weapons, engaged in expressive violence, and humiliation and torture of victims."

"That would be great professor. I'll text you my email address as soon as we get off the phone," Jeannie said.

"Another thing Jeannie, you're correct about the time frames between kills. This maniac is battling urges now that we can't experience. He needs to kill, and the greed motivation is starting to become a non-essential element to his crimes. He knows right from wrong, but if you catch him in the act, he won't surrender. He'll vent his rage on you for interfering with his lust for blood."

Jeannie realized after she got off the phone that she had spent almost forty-five minutes talking to her mentor/friend. She quickly called the San Jose Dispatch center and left a message for Farnworth that she was running late; and if possible, could he push the meeting back an hour or two. She wasn't expecting an answer, but felt better knowing she was free of the commute pressure.

She then called Darcy, her IT go-to person at the bureau. "Hi, Jeannie. How goes it down there in San Jose?" She asked upon answering her phone.

"I'm starting to feel some traction, but there's still a long way to go," Jeannie responded. "I'm wondering if you could do me a favor?" Jeannie gave a detailed report of the killings--their locations, body mutilations and so forth--and asked if Darcy she could do some digging and come up with related type murders in the United States.

CHAPTER FIFTEEN

Feeling she was on a roll, Jeannie called the number she found for the History Department at the University of California in Berkeley. She was bounced around several times on calls until she finally reached Susan Atkins, an Assistant Dean overseeing the History department within the college. After identifying herself, Atkins, acting as if she were cooperating with the enemy, finally said she felt the most appropriate and knowledgeable person for Jeannie was retired professor of antiquities, Dr. Lawrence Caldwell. She added however, that she had not conversed with Dr. Caldwell in years and did not know if he were still alive or if the phone number she gave Jeannie were still active. "Thank you," Jeannie said, but Atkins hung up with no reply.

"Bitch," Jeannie said to herself as she hung up, glancing at her watch. There was time for one more call. She dialed the number given to her and waited.

On the fourth ring a gentleman answered the phone with a hardy "Hello."

"Hello. I am trying to reach Dr. Caldwell," Jeannie began.

"You've reached him, but please just call me Lawrence. How can I help you? Before you answer, if this is a political fundraising ploy, I will be hanging up."

Jeannie laughed to herself. Most of the time when she did not recognize an incoming phone call, she did not answer since most were irritating political calls or some dumb solar company calling. She immediately noticed a deep English accent, and knowing he was retired, she was already trying to picture what Dr. Caldwell looked like.

"Lawrence, my name is Jeannie Loomis, and I'm the Assistant Special Agent in charge of the San Francisco FBI. I got your number from a faculty member at U.C. Berkeley. Do you have a few minutes so I can discuss the nature of my call?

"My or my, I didn't realize they still remembered me there," came his reply. "Those were good time, Agent Loomis. I taught at the university for thirty-six years before I was given my walking papers." He cleared his throat before continuing. "I taught courses in military science, historical weaponry, and even some archeology. It always amazed me how, through generations of war, we produce more and more efficient ways to kill each other."

"Did you retire, Lawrence?" Jeannie asked.

"No. If I had my way I'd still be teaching and loving it. No, society--or I should say our institutions of higher learning—have felt little need to continue educating our students in history related subjects. I don't think my former university even offers courses in American history now, much less World History come to think about it. No, today our colleges and universities are simply interested in the money. I've seen thousands of students now burdened with exorbitant amounts of student debt after wasting five to six years obtaining bachelor's degrees in psychology, theatre arts, fashion design, gender studies, fashion design, sociology, liberal arts, fine art, and so on that will never materialize into a good paying job.

"Some of these areas require much more education than just a bachelor's degree, as you probably know. Students who study theatre arts don't realize until it's too late that you don't need a bachelor's degree to act, and you definitely don't need one to get hired for what's often a low-paying job. Please, don't get me started on the movement toward Gender Study degrees. A gender studies degree on its own is pretty useless because it doesn't prepare you for any particular career path.

"I'm sorry, you hit a trigger regarding my bitterness toward education after dedicating my whole life to it. But that's the reason I was released. I actually heard some of my students say that history had already happened, so why study it. Can you believe that? I got a nice pension, so guess I should be thankful."

"You would have gotten along quite well with my father," Jeannie responded. "Before he passed away he would go off when he saw a student interviewed on television who obviously didn't have a clue about U.S. history or the Constitution. "God help our nation," he would say. My mom would just shake her head and say she pitied the next generation. Anyway, as soon as I asked the dean for the name of their most knowledgeable instructor on weaponry, she recommended you."

Lawrence paused, and Jeannie speculated he was still thinking about his former university position. "What can I do for you Agent Loomis…Jeannie? I hope you're not calling for a grade change. A little late for that," he said with a chuckle. "You asked if I had time? Agent Loomis, physically I'm fine, but bored out of my mind. You're already the most exciting phone call I've had in quite a while. Please go on."

Jeannie laughed. "Well, Dr. Caldwell, I need your help. I'm heading a task force for the San Jose Police Department and we're having a hard time identifying a murder weapon that might have been used. I'm hoping your knowledge on the subject might aid us in our investigation. Sadly, at this time I don't have funds to pay you for your effort, but believe me, if you can help us catch the suspect I'll do anything in my power to reimburse you."

"I see. I'm naturally flattered that you reached out to me," the professor said. "Boy, sounds like a big caper. I'm well compensated for my years of service to the university, so please don't worry about reimbursement. In fact, this is the most exciting thing that's happened for several years. Hearing about the wounds probably won't help. Do you have photos you could legally share with me? You know the old adage, a picture is worth a thousand words."

"Yes, professor. I do. Do you have an email address I can use to send what I have for review?" Jeannie asked.

"I'll bet it surprises you that an 80-year-old actually does have an email address," he said, chuckling. "Let me read it off to you."

Still conscious of the time, Jeannie opened her laptop and quickly sent an email containing several attachments. "OK, you should be receiving them shortly. I'm a little pressed for time, so if it's all right with you, I'd like to call you at noon today and get your take on the likely weapon. What we do know thus far is that the weapon isn't your ordinary hammer. The coroner's office quickly eliminated that possibility. Also, the suspect was able to penetrate through the skull on the first strike, so he's able to generate a lot of power. Are you sure I'm not intruding? I know I'm asking a lot."

"Nonsense young lady. As I said, I'm feeling the Sherlock Holmes in me starting to stir. Anytime today would be fine. Can I ask you a question, however?"

"Sure," Jeannie said, glancing again at her wristwatch.

"Does this have to do with those ghastly murders of poor defenseless elderly people down there? The one the fake news is calling the mutilator?"

"Yes, Lawrence," Jeannie answered. "You understand, there's very little I can tell you about our active investigation, but since I'll be listing you as a consultant, I feel comfortable discussing some of the case with you, providing you keep it confidential."

"Yes, yes, of course. You can count on my confidentiality, Agent Loomis."

"Please, just call me Jeannie. I'll call you as close to noon as possible."

"Can I ask you one other quick question, Jeannie? I know I'm getting ahead of myself, but my creative juices are starting to flow again. Was it a striking weapon or a swinging weapon? In other words, do you visualize the weapon as a knife, a dagger, or something more along the lines of a sword, a club, or even a battle axe?"

"Right now, if I had to speculate I'd lean toward a swinging instrument like a battle axe," Jeannie replied. "I don't feel a blade--you know, a knife or a sword--could do that much damage to the brain cap."

"Well, actually, some of the knives used by our military are strong enough to penetrate a human skull, but I digress," Lawrence added. "One final question, since I know you're pressed for time. Let's assume it's a striking instrument, and since you feel it's a swinging weapon, do you feel the suspect is right or left-handed and does he use one hand or two? Are the wounds from piercing, crushing, or cutting?"

"I'm guessing at this stage that the suspect uses one hand. I can't answer whether he's right or left-handed. The wounds are piercing, penetrating, and three to four inches deep," Jeannie answered.

"This is all very interesting. I'll first review my library of ancient swinging weapons and then visit a few museums tomorrow. Next, I'll start hitting hardware and sporting goods stores. Thanks so much for putting your faith in me, Jeannie. I look forward to talking to you later." Following goodbyes, Jeannie hung up and with a smile on her face thought, *Boy, this guy's really getting into this.*"

CHAPTER SIXTEEN

"Ready for dinner?" Ismail's wife asked as she entered the kitchen where Ismail was sitting, looking at notes on the kitchen table. He did not answer. "Meu amor, I am talking to you." Finally, Ismail looked up. "We need to talk Izzy. You're not eating. You're losing weight and you're no longer paying any attention to me. Is it because you don't like my cooking anymore or that I am not attractive to you because I can't get rid of these extra five pounds?" she asked, grabbing the sides of her stomach.

Ismail stood. "No, no, babe. It's not you at all. It's this case. We just can't get a break and cops are dying--all on my watch. He pulled his wife toward him and gave her a long squeeze and passionate kiss.

"That's better," she said. She grabbed his left hand and motioned for him to sit while she did the same.

"You told me once that cops only catch the dumb ones. When I asked what you meant by that, you said that most of the time criminals make at least one mistake, and that's how you catch them. I'm sure that eventually this guy will also make an error and you'll be able to arrest him."

"Unfortunately, it is not just one person, it's a team," Ismail responded.

"I think that's even better," she replied. "I know I'm not an FBI agent, but if you have two people committing crimes together, there should be an increased chance that one of them will screw up, right? I also think that you miss Jeannie. When you two work together on a case, you seem to feed off of each other. Have you talked to her about this case?"

"Yes, but she's working on a horrific case with the San Jose Police Department, and she's placed her trust in me," Ismail answered.

"Ismail, Jeannie loves you. You two have worked together for how many years now? Look at all those big cases you two have solved. She believes in you and trusts you. You're working all these long hours, and maybe you need to take a break. Just a short one to refocus, and maybe during the break one of the two assholes will mess up and give you that break you're looking for."

Ismail glanced at his wife and agreed. He then notices her black bra strap next to the collar of her blouse and felt a stir. "Where are the kids?" he asked.

Getting a smile on her face, she replied, "They won't be home for an hour."

"Well, you know that old proverb, all work and no play makes Ismail a dull boy, or something like that." They rose from the table and walked briskly toward their bedroom with Ismail already starting to feel better. Halfway up the stairs he grabbed his wife's butt cheek.

"Izzy, you're so bad."

"No, Meu amor, you're about to see how good I am."

On Saturday as Ismail and his team continued to work on their investigation, in another part of the city, Anita Bryant, a 19-year-old black woman, entered her boyfriend's apartment. Calling out to him, she heard someone grunting in the direction of the bathroom. She placed her purse on a chair and walked toward the sound. When she rounded the corner of the hallway, she saw her boyfriend using a small pair of pliers, struggling with his braces over the blood covered basin.

"What are you doing?" she asked as she stood at the entrance to the bathroom. "Get out of here," came his response as he kicked the door shut.

Jeannie arrived at the police department for the briefing almost one and a half hours after it had been scheduled. She went to Farnworth's office ready to apologize but found it empty. "We had another one," announced Anne Lamontt, Farnworth's secretary. "I'm supposed to call a uniformed officer and get you to the scene ASAP."

As expected, the kill site was another rural farmhouse secluded from the main road by several acres of cherry trees. As Jeannie approached the porch area, she was met by Lt. Farnsworth.

"Sorry I'm so late," Jeannie apologized. "I had some important phone calls to make. I hope you got my phone call indicating I'd be late."

"No, I didn't get the message because of this," he said motioning toward the residence. "We've been out here since seven fifteen this morning."

"How bad?" Jeannie asked.

"Probably the worst. Two adults and two little kids."

"Two kids?" Jeannie asked, in a state of surprise and disgust.

"If I'm around when this sick fuck is found, he's not going to have a court date. It'll be a date with the coroner," Farnsworth replied while escorting Jeannie into the house where Jeannie was greeted by several investigators who had attended her first presentation.

"Mercer. Give Agent Loomis a walk through and tell her what we know so far. I'll meet you back at the station later," Farnsworth said as he left.

"Brace yourself," said Detective Mercer. "The first two victims are little ones, and they're just inside the entrance in the front room." Jeannie, following his lead, put on shoe coverings and gloves. They walked into the small entrance that led to the front room off to the right. There, lying on the floor next to each other face up were twin girls, maybe five-years-old.

Both were nude and holding hands. No body parts had been removed. Jeannie immediately noticed wire wrapped around each of the little girls' throats, the ligatures so tight they inflicted bloody wounds.

Seeing enough, Jeannie and Mercer proceeded down the hallway to the master bedroom. Blood was everywhere, on the walls, the ceiling and the bedding. Lying together were two elderly individuals whom Mercer identified as Mr. and Mrs. Miller. Mr. Miller appeared to receive the worst of the blows to the head and face. Both eyeballs had been removed and several teeth were lying on his chest. His penis was missing as well as his hands.

Mrs. Miller had additional blood behind her head. The suspect must have first hit her from behind and then turned her over, Jeannie thought. Her eyes and breasts had been removed. Although not scalped, her hair had been cut off, divided, and placed on both sides of her head. "The suspect is starting to change his M.O., however slightly," she said to Mercer who nodded in agreement.

"The kitchen is next," Mercer said as they retraced their steps through the hallway. A dinner plate on the kitchen table held Mr. Miller's penis and one of Mrs. Miller's breast. It appeared to Jeannie that the suspect had eaten some of the remains. A frying pan on the stove evidenced cooking oil residue and one eyeball. "He's starting to lose it," Jeannie said, heading to the front door as evidence technicians arrived. The uniformed officer said nothing as he drove her back to the station.

Lt. Farnworth had rescheduled the earlier briefing to 2:00 p.m., giving Jeannie time to gather her thoughts about the presentation. A "roach coach" was parked outside the P.D., so Jeannie purchased a burrito and soda and returned to her desk. Having finished what she needed to do at her desk, she thought it was close enough to noon to recall Dr. Caldwell. He answered on the first ring this time.

"Hello Agent Loomis. Right on time."

"Please, call me Jeannie."

"Oh, I'm sorry, Jeannie. I examined your photos with great interest. Let me tell you upfront that I haven't identified the weapon. I've gone through my books and stopped at two museums so far, and although I found a few ancient weapons that could've penetrated the skull, I feel we're looking for a modern weapon or tool. Looking at the photos, I don't feel the wounds were caused by an ancient weapon. No, there were a few that came close, but as they used to say, no cigar. After I finish this call with you, I'll be visiting some home improvement stores, and I have two sporting goods stores in mind as well. I want to see if my hunch is correct."

"What's your hunch, Lawrence?"

"Well, if I'm correct, the object that caused these traumas is more like an axe or pick, but not the kind you'd purchase at a hardware store. No. It would be a special type of object." Following a pause, he continued. "God, this is actually thrilling to me, Jeannie. If possible, I'd like to do more follow-up, and if the delay doesn't hurt your investigation, I'd like to get back to you in two days."

"That would be fine Lawrence. Please don't overdo it. Your health is more important."

"Oh Jeannie, if anything this case is invigorating my health. I'll call you in two days."

After completing her presentation notes, Jeannie still had 20 minutes to kill, so she recalled Dr. Washington. "Hello Jeannie. I was hoping for an update," he said upon answering. "He killed again?"

"Yes, and it was bad. Two adults and two little girls. Fifteen dead so far. He used the same MO (Modus Operandi). The point of entry was a bedroom window. He removed a windowpane again. Apparently, the little twins were sleeping in a bedroom separate from their grandparents. They didn't die from brunt forced trauma. Instead, they were strangled to death with baling wire. No mutilations. They were laid out next to each other and holding hands.

The adult male received the worst of the head beating, and his penis and hands were severed. The female's hair was cut this time, not scalped. Both breasts and eyes were removed. In the kitchen we found a frying pan that had been used to cook partial remains with some parts left on a kitchen plate. Looks like he consumed most of them."

There was silence between Jeannie and Dr. Washington until he spoke. "After we spoke, I contacted a few colleagues that I still keep in touch with and generically discussed the case you're working on. I sincerely hope that what we came up with collectively will help you in your pursuit of this maniac.

"I think what you have, Jeannie, is a person who was not only physically abused in his early youth, but sexually abused as well. It goes without saying that there was also emotional abuse in a very dysfunctional home. He was probably subjected to numerous acts of torture, the perpetrator being his father or father figure. His mother was weak or too cowardly to step in, and was thus an enabler. We feel that many of the classic symptoms of serial killers were present in their earlier formative years--bed wetting, animal dissections and so on.

"Somehow, he broke away from the abuse. He may have just fled, joined the military, or even killed both of his parents. It will be interesting to hear what you learn once he's identified and captured. It's not unusual in these kinds of cases that subjects eventually undergo a psychic break and vividly relive their former harsh life and take their revenge out on other individuals. As I told you many times when you were my gifted graduate student, that although we call the field of psychology a science, it's sometimes just a guessing game until we actually get within the head of the offender. I don't think he's satisfying some sexual urge in his kills.

"Our hypothesis is that the individual you should be looking for is a loner, possibly a transient, and more specifically a farm laborer or possibly an illegal. That's probably not politically correct to speculate these days, but I'm old school, and if you're here illegally you're an illegal, but I'm getting off point.

"We feel that the clubbing victims receive are the killer's initial release of anger. Once they're killed, he takes his time and proceeds to remove body parts that have significant meaning to him. That, you'll determine upon his arrest.

"The positioning of corpses is very important to him. Here, and my colleagues all agree, he's showing a representation of his father and mother. This coincides with the removal of the male's penis--the sexual abuse he received from his father.

The breast removals are in retaliation of his mother for not stopping the abuse. In other words, she nourished him when he was an infant through breast feeding, but then abandoned him when he started growing up and the abuse started. We haven't come up with a consensus that explains the removal of eyes. I hope I haven't bored you with our hypothesis."

"Not at all, Doctor Washington. In fact, you've helped me answer some of the questions I've had regarding the killer's motivations, and now I can share that with my team. I don't know how I can ever make it up to you."

"Jeannie, you already have. It was sincerely an honor to link up with you again. The cases you've solved with the FBI have stroked my ego. Maybe some of the things I taught you created who you are today. Please let me know how the case turns out. We old academicians like to get together to reminisce and gossip, and this case you brought to me is the hottest subject we've had in a long time. We feel like we're a version of the Murder Club out there in San Francisco--you know, the one James Patterson uses in some of his books. Well, we now consider ourselves the Men's Murder Group. Keep us posted."

"I will, Dr. Washington."

CHAPTER SEVENTEEN

Dr. Caldwell (Lawrence) visited several other museums in the area, but none of the ancient weapons appeared capable of producing the wound shape he saw in photos Jeannie sent him. His next two stops were at a Lowe's and Home Depot stores, but what he found lead him to eliminate traditional hammers, picks and axes, so he continued his search in a sporting goods outlet, Alberts Sporting Goods in Berkeley.

The store was not as glamorous as a Big 5 or Dick's, but Lawrence needed a place to start. A grossly overweight male behind the counter asked, "What can I do for you, pops?" Lawrence already formed a dislike of the employee who gave him a visual going-over.

"I was hoping you could help me identify a particular tool." He opened his briefcase and started taking out a drawing he made after analyzing the wound photos Jeannie sent.

"Look Pops. We're not a hardware store. We specialize in athletic equipment. You want tools, go check out Home Depot. I think you're a little old to think about taking up a sport, don't you?" He started to walk away.

"Sir, I'm working as a consultant with the FBI and would like to show you a drawing in hopes your vast knowledge of athletic equipment might help identify the tool in question." In his younger days, he would have probably flipped off the employee and left in a huff.

"No shit. The FBI don't have no age restrictions, huh?"

Lawrence let that comment pass and laid his drawing on the counter. "We're looking for a weapon that may look something like this, judging from the victims' wounds."

"Look pops, I don't have time for this shit." He turned, opened a drawer, and pulled out a book about one and a half inches thick. "Here, you can have this old catalog and search to your heart's content." He threw the book on the counter and walked away. Lawrence did not say thank you; he picked up the catalog and left the store. *Probably has college debt after earning his gender studies degree*, he thought, exiting the store.

He spotted a Black Bear restaurant about a block down from the sporting goods store and decided that since it was almost 11 a.m., he might as well stop and get something to eat while perusing the catalog. A young female waitress greeted him at the door. "Hello. Just one?" she asked.

She seated Lawrence at a corner table and handed him a menu. While he checked out the food items, she returned with a glass of water. "Would you like a few more minutes?" she asked.

"No, I think I'll have the hot turkey sandwich with mashed potatoes and gravy, and maybe a slice of your chocolate pie for dessert. Oh, and a cup of coffee--decaf."

The waitress immediately returned with a cup of coffee and a small container of cream. "Sugar and sweetener are there," she said, pointing to a receptacle with intermixed packets. "I'll be back soon with your meal."

While mixing a pack of Equal and a small amount of cream in his coffee, Lawrence looked at the cover of the catalog. There were pictures of tents, sleeping bags, fishing rods and reels, as well as canoes. The back page showed athletic shoes as well as baseball gloves and clothing. Opening to the table of contents, he found what he was looking for, a section labeled, Hiking and Climbing Gear, listing the ten finest backpacking hatchets and axes. He dispensed with those that did not have a triangular shaped head. He found the M48 Tactical Tomahawk Axe of interest since it was very lightweight, packable and portable, but it did not have a triangle striking head. Furthermore, critiques down rated it, stating that if too much pressure were used while striking, the handle would break.

When his food arrived, he rearranged the place settings so he could continue looking through the catalog while eating. Very few picks were shown and none came close to what he was looking for. By the time he was ready to move onto the chocolate pie, he was ready to give up on the catalog, finding nothing useful.

His next stop was Glades Athletic Supply near a shopping mall in Walnut Creek. *I sure hope I don't run into another asshole*, he thought as he entered. The store smelled of canvas, obviously coming from the numerous erected tents on the showroom floor. "Hello, how can I help you?" asked an elderly lady who was still in excellent shape in Lawrence's opinion.

"I hope you can help me. My name is Lawrence Caldwell, which should mean nothing to you. I'm working as a consultant with the FBI."

"Wow! FBI. You're not an agent, are you?" she asked while containing a polite laugh. "My name is Glades. I'm the owner."

"No, afraid not. I think their training academy in Quantico would kill me," he replied with a smile as he opened his briefcase, pulling out the drawing and laying it on the counter in front of Glades. He explained that he was searching for a tool that might look similar, and then showed another drawing of the wounds it would produce if it were used as a weapon.

"Well, right off the bat I can tell you these wounds didn't come from a claw hammer, or even your standard garden pick. This shape here," she said while pointing to the wound drawing, "looks like a square spike tapering to a sharp point. Plus, you have to factor in that it's arched. No, you're not going to find a tool like this in a hardware store. "

"Yes, exactly. So far, I've not found any tool that matches these wounds," Lawrence replied. "I did find this at a DIY store in Oakland." He pulled a bricklayer's hammer out of his briefcase and placed it on the table.

"Now this is more like it," Glades said. She picked it up and made hammering motions with it. "You're close, but it doesn't seem to curve downward enough when you compare it to the drawings. Look, I have to get home early today to take care of my grandkids. Can I make copies of your drawings and sleep on it tonight? Maybe we could meet for coffee tomorrow morning and do some more brainstorming. What do you think?"

Lawrence quickly realized that it had been years since he actually went out and met a lady, so without hesitation he accepted. "Where would you like to meet?" he asked.

"There's a small local restaurant on High Street. Maybe we can meet there at seven o'clock tomorrow morning. Do you know where it is?" Glades asked.

"I do indeed, and seven sounds wonderful. Thank you so much. You've been a lot of help."

Glades took the documents and Lawrence heard her making copies in her small office off the main sales floor. “Here you go,” Glades said, handing Lawrence the drawings. “I have some ideas, and if I can get my damned grandkids to bed early, I can start my little investigation. By the way, are you married?”

CHAPTER EIGHTEEN

Fighting frustration, Ismail decided to call Jeannie. "Hey boss, how's it going down there in San Jose? Have the serial case all wrapped up?" Ismail asked with a teasing snicker.

"I wish! How's your investigation progressing?" Jeannie replied.

"Not going anywhere. It's like a clogged toilet. You know that once you remove the blockage, things will flow. We just need a break--something we can use that will steer us in the right direction. How about you?" Ismail asked.

"I tell you Ace, sometimes I get a feeling we're close, and then it's the proverbial two steps forward, one step back," Jeannie lamented. "I think we now have a good profile of the perp, but nothing on his identity. I just got off the line with Dr. Washington. He was my Ph.D. program mentor, and he's amazing. Have you ever read any of the Women's Murder Club novels by James Patterson?"

"I think so. Are those the novels where a SFPD homicide detective has a bunch of female friends that meet and discuss some of her ongoing investigations?" he asked. "They do a lot of brainstorming and that helps the main protagonist solve the case."

"Yeah, those're the ones," Jeannie confirmed. "Well, after a conversation with him where I discussed the case, he made contact with a bunch of former psychologists and psychiatrists. These are doctors still considered tops in their fields. Anyway, he now calls them the Men's Murder Club, and after meeting recently they gave me a very detailed diagnoses of what we're dealing with down here. Who the hell needs LinkedIn, huh?"

"Well hell! Maybe I should call him and discuss my damn case. We're not making any progress as it is. Do you think he'd mind?" Ismail asked.

"Oh, hell no. He'll be the hit of their next get-together, bringing in a brand-new case. Let me give you his phone number," she said.

"Do you think he'll tell me any juicy things about his former graduate student?" Ismail again teased.

"Shut up perve," Jeannie retorted. "Here's his number."

The time arrived for Jeannie's long anticipated presentation to the task force. She entered the room without notes or computer, grabbed a bottled water from the rear table and waited until Lt. Farnsworth called the group to order. He was somber in his opening, referring to their absence of leads in the earlier Miller's residence slaughter. Jeannie recognized both his demeanor and that of the assembled officers as signs of frustration and helplessness. She witnessed the same thing when she took over the Marin County Koufax serial case. He concluded his remarks, then turned to Jeannie who took that as a request to take over.

Instead of using the podium, Jeannie leaned against the front table and placed her hands together, interlocking her fingers. "I wish I could make an announcement that I have single-handedly identified the killer, but that's not the case. As I said before, it will take our combined experiences and gut instincts to solve this case.

"My partner, Agent Ismail Flores, and I have a saying when a case is not progressing as fast as we wish. One of us will say to the other, we only catch the dumb ones." Everyone in the room laughed, perhaps to rid the negativity of chasing a ghost.

"First, I want to say that I was very impressed with the presentations you made. I gleaned a lot of valuable information from your narratives and crime scene photos. I've located an individual who's an expert in weapons identification and is currently trying to identity the type of tool used by the suspect. I'm hoping it will be a unique tool which, in turn, will lead us in the right direction.

"Secondly, with the help of others far more knowledgeable than me, I've created a more in-depth psychological profile of the person we're looking for. After I give you this information, I want you to use it when talking to your informants, as well as share it with patrol working the streets. Someone out there knows this individual, but doesn't realize it yet. We'll help them.

"Here's my workup so far. The suspect is probably in his late twenties or early thirties, and probably a Latino and a loner. He's more than likely uneducated and goes from farm to farm looking for work--seasonal work if you will. He had a horrific home life where he was sexually and physically abused. The trauma he inflicts on his male victims is probably due to the physical abuse he received from his father or male figurehead.

"The females represent his mother, and for reasons we don't know, he's taking revenge against her when he kills female victims. His English will be sufficient to get by, but again, he's probably uneducated. The suspect is between 5'9" and 6'0 and has a muscular build. More than likely, he's here illegally. Once we get more information, ICE will be a great source to contact. He knew his victims and had a cursory amount of knowledge about their normal daily routine and the valuables kept in their homes.

"His move into cannibalism is a tough one to diagnosis. Mental health professionals call this type of illness Erotophonophilia, a fancy name for a fucked up, sick individual."

Laughter filled the room after the last remark, and it continued for several minutes. Jeannie used the time to take another gulp of water, then resumed her presentation. "The cannibalism appears to be part of the suspect's psychosis, and the recent uptick in his kills is part of his psychotic break.

"Psychosis may result from of a psychiatric illness like schizophrenia. In other instances it may be caused by a health condition, medications, or drug use. Other possible symptoms he may be experiencing include delusions, hallucinations, talking incoherently, and agitation. The person with this condition usually isn't aware of his or her behavior. Treatment may include medication and talk therapy or a nine millimeter slug. I didn't say that did I?"

The laughter this time was even greater than before.

"OK, as they say in our high-tech world, now is the time for action items. As I stated earlier, I have an expert working on identifying the weapon used in the slayings. Once I get something back from him, I'll forward it to each of you."

She turned to Lt. Farnsworth and asked if someone could put together a global email for all present so as information was passed on to her, she could forward it on to them. Farnsworth looked at his secretary who said it would be done by the end of the day.

Jennie continued, "Based on our new psychological profile, we need to reinterview as many farmers and ranchers in the area as we can to learn how they procure workers for their spread. I have a nosy neighbor whom I love dearly, and who may have unknowingly provided a possible avenue for us to follow. When she was a kid, she used to go with her family to pick apricots at a relative's orchard. She told me that when harvest time came around, her relatives always had to find additional workers to collect the fruit before it spoiled. With that in mind, we need to visit DIY stores in the county, especially in the morning hours when laborers gather for jobs. Talk to the contractors present and see if anyone fits the profile I just gave you.

"The laborers you interview need to be given some of the profile information I just shared with you. Ask them, especially those who have worked at any of the victims' farms, if they recall others who came in late to help with the harvest.

"Finally, I know that all of you are putting in tons of hours working this case. We're all stressed, but remember that our families at home are also stressing with us. Try to carve a little time out of your hectic schedule and give them some quality time.

"I was asked by my late fiancé what love was." Jeannie felt a lump in her throat, so she grabbed the water bottle and took another gulp. "I told him I had asked by mom the same question when I was about ten-years-old. She told me that when two people are together and feel complete, they experience love. When they are apart, they do not feel complete. Your family's love is the same. It's not complete when you're absent, so please spend some quality time with them.

"I think we're due for a break, but the times between kills will shrink. His lust for killing is almost overwhelming. Patrols need to be increased in areas he considers hunting grounds. Let's hope and pray he makes a mistake so we can take him off the streets. Thank you."

Lt. Farnsworth returned to the podium as Jeannie took her seat. "Alright, Agent Loomis has given us a ton of avenues to follow and restart our investigation. Get out there and hit the bushes. You'll start receiving updates from either Agent Loomis or me, hopefully by this afternoon. Let's catch him before he strikes again."

CHAPTER NINETEEN

Jeannie read the submitted crime reports for the last killings, but did not learn anything new. Calling it a day and telling Farnsworth she was heading home to beat the commute, she climbed into her bureau car. Before she had time to start the engine, her cellphone went off, displaying an unfamiliar number, but obviously from the East Bay. "This is Agent Loomis," she said.

"Hello Agent Loomis, I mean Jeannie. I hope this is a good time to call you. This is Lawrence. I think I have some good news. I believe I know the type of weapon used in the killings. I don't have the particular brand nor know who manufactures them, but I think we're on the right track."

Jeannie told him she was trying to stay ahead of the traffic on her way home and that as soon as she arrived, she would return his call. She could hardly wait to hear what he had discovered.

The damned commute was still hell. She made a mistake and tried to take a surface street, Mission Blvd, to bypass the mess on Highway 880, but that plan backfired. An hour and ten minutes later she arrived home--tired, hungry, angry, and in need of a shower. Fortunately, Delores was not hanging around outside ready to pounce on her. With a sigh of relief, she quickly entered the sanctity of her home.

A quick refrigerator check produced half of a Subway sandwich. "That and a can of Campbell's turkey noodle soup will do it," she said to herself and leading to her singing, "Soup and sandwich, soup and sandwich. Have your favorite Campbell soup and sandwich. Anytime or weather, soup and sandwich go together." She remembered how her mom used to sing the song from the Campbell soup commercial. "Thinking about you Mom," she said out loud. She placed the sandwich on the granite countertop and opened the can of soup, pouring its contents into a microwave safe soup bowl and setting the timer for two minutes.

Jeannie removed her weapon and placed it next to the sandwich, the Campbell's soup song still in her head, but degrading to a hum. She climbed the stairs to her master bedroom, undressed and stepped into a hot shower. After toweling off, she put on her sweat bottoms and top. Feeling refreshed, she returned to the kitchen, took the soup bowl from the microwave and grabbed the sandwich. It felt good to sit down in her dining room, eat, and say hello to her fish. Partially finishing the sandwich and soup, she picked up her phone and entered Lawrence's number.

"Hello Jeannie," he said. "I hope you feel better after battling that traffic. I tell you, even before I retired I could see it getting worse."

"I remember as a kid being driven by my mom and dad. You only had to avoid the freeways from seven 'till eight in the mornings, and from five 'till six in the evening, but that's not the case any longer," Jeannie replied. "I'm anxiously waiting to hear what you've discovered in your search. By the way, again, I greatly appreciate what you're doing for us."

"The pleasure's all mine," he said. "I visited a few more stores here in Berkeley, but had little luck. So I expanded my search area to include Oakland, Concord, and finally Walnut Creek. In Walnut Creek I made some progress at a sporting goods store.

I found the store's owner to be a delightful elderly lady who was very knowledgeable. I cautioned her before I showed the wound photos, but she had been a surgical nurse during the Vietnam War, so wasn't shocked at all. Well, Glades, that's her name, immediately ruled out common claw and ballpeen hammers as tools that could cause those wounds. She got out a magnifying glass and looked closely at the wounds. She thought the tool used was likely an axe, but not an ordinary axe. She wants to think further about it tonight and will get back to me tomorrow."`

"An axe! Not a pick?" Jeannie asked, nearly choking on a bit of sandwich. "Sorry, Lawrence, I hope you don't mind. I'm eating a sandwich and soup while we talk." The mention of an axe surprised her.

"Not a problem," he said in an understanding tone. "After I left Glades--with whom I might add, I have a future coffee date with tomorrow morning--I went to a large sporting goods store in Walnut Creek." Chuckling to himself, he continued. "The salesperson there agreed they looked like axe inflicted wounds, but he didn't provide anything useful. I'm hoping Glades comes up with something."

"You devil, you," Jeannie said. "A coffee date, huh?"

"Yes. Well anyway, I just wanted to let you know about my progress." Jeannie could not help but notice how quickly Lawrence evaded the dating comment.

"An axe? What would an illegal orchard laborer be doing with an axe? Do you think those sporting goods salespeople may have meant hatchet?" she asked.

"I'm sorry, Agent Loomis. Remember, I don't know the suspect's relationship to the weapon or the person you're seeking."

Feeling she had somehow offended Lawrence, Jeannie quickly replied. "No, I'm sorry Lawrence. The statement wasn't meant for you. I usually have a partner whom I bounce things off of, and I guess I did the same with you. I apologize. I'm just trying to fit the possession of an axe with the psychological makeup of our suspect. We believe he's a migrant worker from Mexico with a limited education, and I can't conceive of him walking around with an axe, but I can imagine a hatchet. Let's wait and see what Glades comes up with."

"Oh, I understand," Lawrence said. "I'd like to make an educated guess however. In one of the sporting goods stores I visited I saw a unique tool I'd never seen before. I was told it was an ice axe. I didn't know you had already figured out the nationality of the suspect, and I agree that one does not usually relate a mountain climbing tool such as an ice axe with a device needed in Mexico.

"I still have a place I want to visit tomorrow after I meet with Glades. It's a specialty shop in San Francisco that's supposed to have a number of ice axes. Will you be at the San Jose Police Department tomorrow afternoon?"

Jeannie assumed he was asking if she would be available so he could call her. She affirmed and told him any time would be fine. They hung up and Jeannie cleaned up the dining room table mess she had created. She sat for a few minutes at the table talking to her fish, especially her favorite, and dashed some food into their domain. "Good night guys and gals. See you in the morning."

Jeannie thought to herself, *Ice axe. How in hell would a fruit picker come up with an ice axe? Huh. Nah, they must have meant hatchet. That makes more sense. Still, it's something to be investigate.* Entering her second bedroom she grabbed a 3" by 4" sheet of heavy paper and wrote, "ice axe—hatchet" followed by a question mark, then taped it alongside other pertinent information about the killings on the whiteboard. *You may not know it yet, you fucker, but I'm closing in on you!*

CHAPTER TWENTY

Anita Bryant gave her boyfriend a few days to cool off, then returned to his apartment. She had not answered or returned his calls since he slammed the bathroom door on her and kicked her out. Finally, she responded to a call and he apologized. She would give him one more chance, but actually it was more like his seventh or eighth chance. Her girlfriend told her to leave the loser, but she stayed because she was in love with him.

When he answered the door she immediately noticed he had successfully removed his braces. His lips were a little swollen and she asked him if he were OK. "Fuck yes, I'm OK! Why the hell didn't you answer my phone calls, you bitch? What if I'd really needed you? Get your butt over her and give me some love."

She tried to resist, but after a hard slap, she gave in to his wishes. As she laid there allowing him to get his rocks off, she saw a chrome plated automatic on an adjacent coffee table.

Jeannie was having a weird dream in which her bedroom closet was about to burst at the seams from an excessive number of stored ET, Cabbage Patch, My Little Pony, Care Bears, Holly Hobby, and a collection of Barbie dolls. Spoiled? Just a little. She still had many of these collectibles, but the dream took place in her childhood bedroom. *My God. This case is getting to me*, she thought. *I need to get a social life after I put this asshole in jail.*

CHAPTER TWENTY-ONE

"Olodumare, most holy one, my creator. Ochosi, the hunter, who I follow and hope to satisfy. It is I, your warrior, who will offer more sacrifices to you this night." He drank directly from a bottle of Jimador Tequila, and after swallowing most of the mouthful, he sprayed what remained onto several lit candles on a small altar, producing bursts of flame.

A small sparrow was trying to escape from a large, upside down emptied plastic Coke bottle from which the top portion had been removed and the opening covered with a piece of cloth. The bird was found with an injured wing and could not fly away. He stood, bowed to the altar, looked at the bird, and then began a ritual of dancing, drumming, and speaking to the orishas.

He picked up a knife from the altar and raised it to the dark sky that had enveloped his homeless encampment which was nothing more than a black sheet of plastic draped over a tree along Highway 680 in San Jose. There were over 100 homeless individuals living in the area, but he preferred isolated. Spitting more Tequila on the candles, he reached into the Coke bottle and grabbed the bird. Holding it on the altar, he removed the animal's head with one quick cut. Blood rained over the wooden altar. Continuing to chant, he dissected the bird's wings and legs and left the body parts on the altar.

He awakened a few hours later, not knowing the time. It was not important. Darkness was all that mattered. Grabbing his tool, he climbed on his motorcycle and drove through the canyon to the Lamont farm. Shutting off the bike some distance from the farmhouse so it would not be audible, and pushing it the remainder of the way, he concealed it behind a large Camellia bush to the rear of the residence. He remembered the bush from when he picked cherries in the large orchard that summer. It was the location he used to spy on the Lamont's and saw their safe through the window.

There were no lights on in the house that he could see from his location, but he was nevertheless quiet while deciding which window to remove. Inside his head he was saying, *Ochosi, are you proud of your servant? Do you see how skillfully I snuck up on their house? The sacrifice I'm about to offer is to you. A sacrifice that I pray will keep the father and mother in damnation forever.*

A bedroom window to a south of the master bedroom was badly in need of new putty, making windowpane removal easy. Upon removal, he listened. The was only silence. Before climbing inside, he lowered his tool inside the bedroom and placed it against the wall. Still no sound. Once inside, he familiarized himself with the farmhouse layout as best he could. He walked down the hallway toward the master bedroom, passing a bathroom.

That is when he heard snoring coming from old man Lamont. There was enough moonlight passing through the window that once he entered the room he was able to see Mrs. Lamont sleeping to the left of her husband. Visions of his father whipping him and placing hot irons on his back and testicles raced through his mind. He saw his mother looking away as he screamed in pain.

He raised the axe high over his head and brought it down with tremendous force. A crushing sound invaded the quiet room. Mrs. Lamont stirred, but did not awaken. Attempts to retrieve the axe was harder than he had experienced in the past, so he climbed onto the bed and place his right knee on old man Lamont's chest. After two attempts he was able to pull the weapon out. He heard a scream coming from Mrs. Lamont who attempted to raise her head from the pillow. He hit her head with the axe, appearing to knock her out and allowing him to return to Mr. Lamont.

"You did not love me. You only wanted me as an object to torture," he said out loud as he again raised the axe and brought it down on the old man's face. Again and again he repeated the blows. His frenzy could not be controlled. All of the abuse and punishment he received from his unloving father was being released, all to satisfy Ochosi who would keep his old man in hell.

His attention turned to Mrs. Lamont. He hit her again, but his tool was saturated with blood, making it hard to grip securely. *What's that sound?* he asked himself, not initially realizing it was a knock at the front door. *Escape! That's what Ochosi would want me to do. That's what a warrior would do.*

He quickly retreated to his point of entry and lowered the axe outside the window. The knocking on the front door continued. Having climbed out of the opening, he ran to the Camilla bush, jumped on his bike, and drove from the house in the darkness without turning on its light. Moonlight guided him.

CHAPTER TWENTY-ONE

The next morning, Jeannie could not process the vibration she sensed in her dream until it dawned on her the cellphone was ringing.

"Loomis," she said, trying to fully awaken.

"Jeannie, it's Farnsworth. We have another one, but this time one of the victims is alive."

Jeannie, using the emergency equipment on her car, flew down Highway 880, formerly called the Nimitz's freeway, and made the drive to San Jose in roughly 18 minutes. The uniformed officer who normally escorted her around the city was waiting. "Where do you want to go first, the hospital or the crime scene?" he asked.

"Is the victim conscious?" she replied with yet another question.

"That, I don't know. Sorry," he answered"

"OK, let's go to the crime scene. Is that where Lt. Farnsworth is?" Jennie asked.

"Yes. He told me to let you decide where you wanted to go first."

The kill site was another farmhouse not much different than the others. By the time Jeannie made her way to the front door, crime scene technicians were already discussing their plan to proceed. To the side was a young adult male talking with a detective standing next to a uniformed officer.

Farnsworth, immerging from the entrance saw Jeannie and said, "Maybe we finally got the break we've hoped for." Jeannie put on protective gear so she would not contaminate the scene and followed Farnsworth inside. "The home is owned by Frank and Mary Lamont. Frank is the deceased. Both are elderly and have lived here for forty-plus years."

Jeannie saw the kitchen immediately upon entering. It appeared clean and orderly. *No frying pan with body parts, thank God*, she thought. A coroner's investigator preparing to leave, told Farnsworth that he had concluded his examination, and that once the crime scene techs were through, he would transport the body to the morgue. As this conversation ensued, Jeannie passed around the examiner in the hallway proceeded toward the master bedroom where she saw a nude male on a blood-soaked bed. His head appeared to have imploded, but his genitals were intact. The pillow next to the victim was also saturated with blood. There was no clipped hair near the pillow in this case. A cursory inspection showed blood still dripping from the ceiling over where the victims slept, obviously splatter from when the suspected raised and lowered his weapon.

Farnsworth entered the room. "Blunt force trauma to the head, but this sick fuck was scared off by the person we're interviewing outside. The guy's car broke down about a quarter mile down the road. His cellphone's battery was dead so he hiked up here to see if he could get help. The porch light was on, so he began knocking, hoping to awaking someone who could help him. That must have spooked our suspect, whom we believe exited through the POI (pointing to a bedroom window). The kid never got a front view of the suspect, but heard what he described as a dirt bike speeding down the road you just used to come here.

"The female victim has nasty wounds on her forehead, but the paramedics feel the blows did not penetrate as deeply as those to the husband. Remarkable, considering the amount of damage done to her spouse. They're more concerned with the trauma at the crown of her head that night have caused brain damage. She was unconscious when transported to the hospital. My detectives are with her now and will let us know when she can talk. Also, thanks to the rain, we found decent tire tracks near the barn where he must have hidden his bike. They're good enough for comparisons later."

The two walked over to the individual being interviewed. Identifying herself, Jeannie asked him if he would mind answering a few additional questions. "Sure, not a problem," came the reply.

"I understand that you didn't get a good look at the subject. Is that correct?" Jeannie asked.

"Yeah. As I told the officer, I knocked on the front door and listened for a response. I heard what sounded like someone making sounds around the side of the house at a window. So I went around the house to see if someone was there. That's when I saw a person come racing out from the barn area on a motorcycle. I couldn't get a good look at him. There was only moon light."

"One more question," Jeannie said. I heard you say he was driving a dirt bike, but now you said a motorcycle."

"I'm sorry," he answered. "I meant a dirt bike. I could tell it was much smaller than a normal motorcycle, and since I drive one myself, I can tell the difference. Another thing, now that I think about it. The bike was way too small for that dude. I mean, it almost looked like the pictures you see of clowns in the circus driving those little bicycles. This was a pretty good sized guy. I don't mean fat either. He was big overall and appeared muscular."

Farnsworth's cell rang and Jeannie could hear part of the conversation. The voice on the phone asked, "Farnsworth, what do you have?"

There was a short pause until Farnsworth said, "OK, Agent Loomis and I will head there now." He hung up and turned to Jeannie. "The victim's groggy, but able to talk. Let's head over there right now. I think you might have been right. I'm feeling hopeful that we might have our first break."

"Come on girl! You need to go to the police. Look what that asshole did to you. Come on. I need to take you to the police. You can't continue to be his punching bag," came the voice on the phone.

"I don't want him to get in trouble," Anita replied to her girlfriend, Latisa. "I still love him."

Latisa continued, "How can you still love him! Look what he did to your face. I wouldn't allow any man to do to me what this fuck has done to you. The next time, that motherfucker is going to kill you, Anita! Is that what you want?"

"Can I just stay a few days at your house? Anita timidly asked. "Then I can decide what I want to do."

Farnsworth and Jeannie entered the Intensive Care unit, and after showing their identification, they were directed down a long hallway where they made a right turn. A uniformed officer was outside the door and corrected his posture when he saw them approach. Before entering, Detective Stewart came out and gave both of them an update.

"Besides some nasty wounds requiring a lot of stitches and a bad headache, she is alert. It's amazing she didn't suffer the same degree of trauma as her husband did. The doctor has given us permission to talk with her, but for no more than twenty minutes. She's on pain killers, but lucid. By the way, the doctor has already told her that her husband didn't make it."

Jeannie and Farnsworth entered the victim's ER room where a second detective was standing. He was someone Jeannie recognized, but could not remember by name. He nodded at Jeannie and Farnsworth, but since he had nothing to offer beyond what he heard Stewart tell them, he left the small ER that was room loaded with noisy medical equipment.

Farnsworth looked at Jeannie who started the conversation by introducing herself and the lieutenant. "Mary, do you feel up to talking with us for a few minutes?" In a soft voice, Mary said she was. "I know you've probably told several officers what happened tonight, but we've been so busy playing catch up that we need you to retell the events of the evening. Is that OK with you?" Mary's eyes began to water, and she reached for a glass of water which Jeannie helped her hold.

Placing the glass on the side table, Mary began to share her recollection. "My husband and I had been asleep for maybe an hour when I heard my husband yell out in pain. I was on my side, and when I turned over, I saw this huge man standing over my husband's chest trying to take a hammer out of my husband's head. I screamed, and that's when he hit me on the top of my head." She reached up to point to the spot, but stopped when she felt the IV in her arm. "I turned and tried to get out of bed, but he hit me again and I guess I passed out. Oh my God! What am I going to do without Sam?" She began to cry, which must have caused her blood pressure to spike. A nurse quickly came into the room and suggested they might have to wrap up the interview soon.

Jeannie asked Mary if she could describe the assailant. "Yes, he was big. He had on a flannel shirt, or at least I think it was a flannel shirt. He stopped hitting me when he heard someone knocking on our front door. I thought he was going to come over and hit me again, but he ran down the hallway. Then I heard a motorcycle start up and the spinning of gravel near the barn. Oh God, there was so much blood. My sweet Sam."

Thanking Mary for her help and bidding her well, Farnsworth and Jeannie left the room just before "Nurse Ratchet" was ready to reenter. "Tomorrow morning, bright and early, we need your best sketch artist in her room for a drawing. If no one's available, let me know and I'll get one from my office," Jeannie said excitedly as they left the hospital.

CHAPTER TWENTY-TWO

Lawrence woke up with a smile on his face. He made sure he had an extra close shave and dashed on a bit of Lomami cologne. He put on his green shirt and green pullover sweater, hoping it would bring out the color of his eyes when he met with Glades. Checked himself one more time in the mirror, he headed out the door for the coffee shop.

When he arrived, he found a cozy corner table and told the waitress he was waiting for someone and that he would order then. He did opt for a cup of coffee in the meantime. Promptly at seven o'clock, Glades arrived. Waving at Lawrence she made her way through the tables to where he was seated. He stood and shook her hand. He couldn't help notice that she had several papers in her hand including his drawings. "You look very nice this morning. I guess your grandkids behaved themselves," he began.

"Please! I think I'll need a full urn of coffee to stay awake today. Those little monsters could sure use a little corporal punishment, but you know how modern parents are. Not like it was in my day. You disrespected my mom, and my dad had something a lot worse than a time out."

The waitress returned with menus. After a few moments of silence while the two quickly scanned the offerings, Glades said she would have the waffles and sausage plate, plus decaf. Lawrence was thinking the same. *Could this be fate*, he wondered. After Lawrence placed their orders, Glades took advantage of the clear table top, put the documents on it and opened them.

"I think I might have something for you," she said. She pushed his drawings to the corner of the table, and smoothed out photos that appeared to come from a catalog similar to what Lawrence had used earlier. "I think this is the type of tool you're looking for," she said. "Looking at your drawings, I kind of knew this had to be a specialty object. Nothing for around the home." She showed him a picture of a F Ralling Kuno ice axe piolet. "This is an old ice axe used in its day for mountain climbing, and from what I read, only dedicated climbers used it. At the time, it was considered you might say, state of the art."

"My God!" Lawrence exclaimed. "There's the triangle we were looking for, and its weight could easily generate a lot of thrust and velocity by an assailant. How did you find it?"

"Well, before I left the shop yesterday afternoon, I went through our contact lists of stores that provide vintage items such as handguns, bows, rifles and camping and hiking equipment. I found a company we did business with a few times that carried vintage mountain climbing gear, and bingo, there she was," Glades said.

"Since it's vintage, how might a person go about purchasing one?" he asked.

"Well, I made a call and found the owner of the store that distributed the catalog and I told him a little lie--that I was working for the FBI, and he kindly gave me the information I wanted. Normally, I'd have to order this from him. He'd search through his contacts--mostly private dealers--and if he found the object, he'd inflate the price and that's how he'd generate income," she explained.

"So, for me to get one of these Kuno ice axes, I'd have to place an order with him?" Lawrence asked. "Gee, I was hoping to quickly pick one up and take it to my FBI contact."

"You're going to owe me big time, mister," Glades said with twinkling eyes. "By chance, a person several months ago wanted to purchase the axe, but after the item came in, the buyer never came back to take it and my contact still has it at the store. And, it's for sale." Glades could see how excited Lawrence was becoming. "Now, here's what I suggest. After our nice breakfast, we drive up to San Francisco, and after you examine it, we buy it."

"That's great. I can't wait to show Jeannie--my contact with the FBI—what's being used in those ghastly murders."

"You never told me," Glades said. "Are the murders happening down in San Jose?"

"Yes," he answered. "Sorry, but there's only so much information I'm allowed to reveal. You understand?"

"Sure, I understand," she said. "I just hope that discovering the weapon goes a long way in solving the case. So, have you ever been married? Do you have any kids?"

CHAPTER TWENTY-THREE

The next morning as Jeannie was fastening her seatbelt and about ready to back out of her garage for the San Jose commute, her cellphone rang. "Loomis," she answered. It was Cindy, Farnsworth's secretary.

"Hi Jeannie. There's an elderly gentleman here to see you named Lawrence. He said he's helping you identifying a weapon."

"Really. OK, give him a cup of coffee and tell him I'll be there within 15 minutes." "It's coming together. I can feel it," she said to her radio.

"He's in your office, Agent Loomis," Cindy said when Jeannie arrived.

Jeannie entered and saw Lawrence seated across from her chair, sipping a cup of tea. "Lawrence, what a nice surprise," she said as she greeted him. "You didn't have to come all the way down here. It's so nice to meet you in person."

"As I told you on the phone, Jeannie. This is the most excitement I've had in a long time."

"Well, maybe you'll have some more excitement with Glades when you meet for dinner," she said with a kidding smile.

"One can only hope," Lawrence replied, realizing he was blushing. Reaching for a brown paper bag he had placed near his chair and handing it to Jeannie, he continued. "I believe with a high degree of certainty that this is the type of tool used as the murder weapon."

Opening the bad, Jeannie saw an axe unlike anything she had ever seen before. It had an obviously old and unique wooden handle, was lightweight and well balanced. While Jeannie examined the axe, Lawrence pulled a piece of paper from his shirt pocket. "What you're holding, Jeannie, is a vintage F Ralling Kuno ice axe piolet, meaning it was made for mountain climbing. I had to ask for its definition. It's also referred to as a Himalay-Pickel which I can only surmise was a nickname given to it by mountain climbers. It was produced by Felix Ralling Hammerworks in a little village called Fulpmers in the Stubai Valley in South Tyrol, Austria. I have actually been there while I was on sabbatical. Very beautiful.

"As you can see, it has a large spoon shaped adze that I measured at two and a half inches wide by four inches long, and ten and a half inches in overall length, pick to adze. It has the classic straight pick style with five teeth for hooking into ice and snow, and historical manufacturer's symbolic markings. Remarkably, it only weighs slightly over one and a half pounds, but if it's raised up and over the head and brought down forcibly it can generate a lot of crushing energy. This particular model is called the Kuno Rainer. The early ones could only be bought in Austria, way before the Internet and eBay. But since this one made it to San Francisco, who knows where your killer got his. I feel extremely confidant, Jeannie, that your forensic scientists will conclude the configurations of this axe precisely match those of your victims' wounds."

Jeannie paused, placed the axe back in the bag, and after staring a few moments at Lawrence finally said, "Lawrence, I don't know what to say. I wish my FBI agents had your investigative talent and your tenacity. You don't know how much your discovery will aid us in our investigation, and how you saved us a tremendous amount of manpower hours. Regardless of how this eventually plays out, there's now a large reward that's been issued for any individual who helps us capture this killer. I will personally do whatever I can to see that you're considered."

"Please Jeannie. Your trust in me is all this old man could want. This was an experience of a lifetime. I just hope you capture him soon. I'll be following the news."

"When we catch him, you'll be the first one I call," Jeannie said.

CHAPTER TWENTY-FOUR

Jeannie walked into Farnsworth's office carrying the axe in the brown paper bag. "You brown-bagging today?" he asked as she entered.

"Yeah, my stomach couldn't take much more of your roach wagon," she answered, placing the bag on his desk. "This I believe, will match the wounds of our victims. This is a copy of the murder weapon used in the killings."

Farnsworth opened the bag and took out the axe. "My God! Imagine a muscular male in a psychotic rage, raising this axe and coming down on a sleeping, defenseless elderly person. Let's go to the coroner right now and see what he says." While they rode to the coroner's office, Jeannie asked if the sketch artist was successful in the Mary Miller interview. Farnsworth opened the leather binder he had place between him and Jeannie and took out a drawing showing a Latino male with eyes dark as night. "Meet our killer," he said as he turned into the morgue's parking lot.

Dr. Maitland was completing an autopsy on a motor accident victim. Jeannie smeared a little Vick's under her nose as soon as she entered the room. She kept a small jar of it in her purse for such occasions. Even Vicks did not totally erase the smell of death, however. Addressing Farnworth, Maitland said, "This must be important." Looking at Jeannie he continued, "We rarely get management down here. They normally send in their detectives to view the show. I'm Doctor Maitland."

"This is Special Agent Jeannie Loomis of the FBI. She's on loan to help us with the mutilator cases," Farnworth said, introducing the two.

"Yes, hello," Jeannie said without offering her hand "We've talked on the phone about the autopsy reports."

"I didn't realize when I talked with you that you're the famous Agent Jeannie Loomis who took out three jihadists teams a few years ago?"

"I don't know about the famous part, but yes, my team did a hell-of-a-job solving those cases," she modestly replied.

"Yes, yes," Maitland said, turning his attention back to Farnsworth. "OK Farnsworth, what brings you down here?" On cue, Farnsworth opened the paper bag and pulled out the ice axe. "Do you think you could do a quick look to see if that's a possible match with our victims wounds?" Dr. Maitland took the axe from Farnsworth, and while inspecting the head of the tool called over his assistant coroner.

"Scott, do me a favor and bring up as many photos as you can on the computer so we can make a preliminary analysis." Without answering Scott, a tall lanky individual who could pass as an undertaker walked over to a computer on a far wall and began searching files. He took a photo of the axe and placed in the data base for a comparison match.

"I've never seen an object like this before. Gee, you could really generate a lot of force with this thing. Right off the bat I can tell you that none of the wounds came from this side of the axe, but this side looks promising. Let's see what our comparison computer analysis indicates." Fifteen minutes later, an excited Jeannie and Farnsworth left the coroner's office with their second big break in the case. Although Jeannie would arrange a more thorough analysis to be conducted by the FBI, Dr. Maitland felt that it matched all of the wounds.

Jeannie asked Farnsworth to assemble the task force for a late afternoon meeting. She wanted to show them the axe and bring everyone up to speed on the progress being made—essentially, a pep talk. She also wanted to list avenues that had to be quickly investigated. Because the murderer's killing spree was interrupted the night before, he would likely be needing to satisfy his lust and urgently searching for his next prey.

Jeannie found a sandwich shop within walking distance of the P.D. and chose to eat her hot roast beef sandwich and diet Dr. Pepper there inside the station. Still eating, she called Ismail to tell him the good news. "Hey boss," he said. "I was just thinking about you. Since you're a big celebrity serial killer extraordinaire, I was thinking you won't be using your office here in the City By The Bay much, so I was thinking of installing a large flat screen and maybe a refrigerator--you know, a mancave for yours truly."

Laughing, Jeannie said, "Look mister, I think with a little more luck we'll be able to wrap up this case down here, and that means I'll be returning. So no. You can't do anything in my office."

"Gee. Touchy, touchy! What's the matter? None of those young hot San Jose Police Detectives hitting on you?" Ismail could barely complete the sentence, trying to suppress a laugh.

"Hey, jerk. I still turn a lot of heads. Besides, I don't have time for romance. Too many bad guys to catch. Anyway asshole, the reason I called was to fill you in about our case. We finally got several breaks," and she outlined them for him.

"Damn it girl! When your hot, your hot. Why don't you send some of that good karma down here? I could sure use it," he lamented.

"Your breaks will come," Jeannie said. "They always do. I won't ask how your investigation is going since you'd be bragging already if you were about to solve it."

"Oh, that hurts. You sure know how to pick on a defenseless little Portaguee being worked to death because his supervisor is in high demand throughout the great wacko state of California. Just promise me you'll stay safe when you catch your suspect, OK? Meanwhile, I'll leave your office alone for now. Hurry on back." With that, Ismail hung up.

I really miss that shit, Jeannie thought as she finished her lunch.

"When it rains, it pours," Farnsworth said as Jeannie was returning to the office from lunch.

"What's up?" Jeannie asked.

"Come with me to interview room number one," he said with Jeannie in tow. "While you were at lunch, a person came in saying that he has some information on the person whose picture is being shown on the local media channels--you know, the sketch. Here we are. "

Farnsworth knocked on the door and Detective Stewart invited them in. Jeannie saw a good-looking young black man sitting on the guest side of a metal desk dressed in business casual. "Sorry, James. This is Lt. Farnsworth, my supervisor, and this is Special Agent Loomis of the FBI. Farnworth said nothing; Jeannie nodded her head.

"Let's start from the beginning so my lieutenant and Agent Loomis can get up to speed." James said he worked at a casino just south of the city toward Morgan Hill as a blackjack dealer, and that he had been employed by the casino for over a year. The first time he saw "Lobo" was when Lobo sat down to play.

"Lobo?" asked Farnsworth. "That has to be a nickname, right?" Jeannie felt that Farnsworth was a little too aggressive during the initial stage of the interview. She personally found it best, and taught her agents to let an interviewee tell their story before asking specific questions.

"Yeah, he goes by Lobo, but I think his real name is Noe Munoz. The first time I saw him, he sat down and had such bad body odor that the person next to him got up and joined another table. I can't help but remember that. He never had a lot of money to gamble with, and he wasn't much of a blackjack player either. The guy really has a short fuse. He came in on Father's Day and sat at my table again. I welcomed him by saying Happy Father's Day, and he became unglued. He jumped out of his chair and said, what the fuck do you mean, so loudly that one of our plainclothes security officers headed to my table. I apologized to him. But man, you could see hate in his eyes. Seeing the security officer approaching, he sat down and remained quiet until I cleaned him out of funds. And another thing, he always seemed to hold back enough money to visit the buffet. I got the impression it was his biggest meal of the week."

"Did he tell you where he lived?" Jeannie asked.

"No, but I got the impression he probably lives outdoors because of his body odor and the bits of leaves and grass I've seen on his shirts and pants. I know he doesn't have a car because one time he told me he was having a few problems with his dirt bike. His hands were filthy, covered with grease and oil. I've only seen him wear two different shirts, and the same with his pants until a few weeks ago when he came in all dressed up. He sat down at my table in a nice off-the-rack suit, but no tie. The top three buttons of his shirt were open, and I could see he was wearing a thick gold chain around his neck. He was also wearing a shiny wristwatch, but I couldn't see the brand, of course."

Jeannie thought about the time frame, and that this appearance change and flash of bling corresponded with the $100,000 theft during the Shanahan murders. A few more questions were asked, but nothing of substance. Jeannie had not noticed Farnsworth texting to someone, but later learned that he had requested an expediated copy of Noe Munoz's driver's license.

As Jeannie was thinking it was about time to conclude the interview, there was a knock on the door. Farnsworth answered and an unknown female handed him a sheet of paper. "Is this Munoz?" he asked, as he slide the paper across the desk to James.

"That's him, without a doubt," came the response he and Jeannie were hoping to hear.

CHAPTER TWENTY-FIVE

Things were moving fast now, just the way Jeannie liked it. After conferring with Farnsworth upon leaving the interview room, she called Ismail. "Hey boss, you got it solved yet?" he asked upon answering his cell.

"I don't want to jinx myself, so I'll wait to brag later," Jeannie responded. "I want to ask if I could enlist Burk and Darcy's help for a few hours starting now? We have a solid suspect, and I need a lot of searches and contacts ASAP."

"Hey, whatever you need. We've got squat here, so why let their talent go to waste," he answered.

"You're still too hard on yourself, Ace. Just like our case here, you'll get a break. You watch!"

A team of two, Burk and Darcy worked at desks placed close together. Previously, they had been assigned to the FBI field office in Roseville and had been victims of the urban terrorist group attack by the Sons and Daughters of Liberty, headed by their notorious leader, Joey. Jeannie was also a victim of that attack. She was pregnant at the time, and the shot she took to the abdomen caused her to lose her fetus. Joey's group was later terminated in a shootout in Concord, California, but he alone escaped. Ricky Pinheiro, Jeannie's fiancé and Ismail Flores' cousin, was killed by a ricocheting bullet during the that shootout. Joey had planned a massive terrorist attack at the Democratic National Convention in Los Angeles, but Jeannie discovered the devices before the deadly virus could be released on the attendees. Joey was captured, sent to prison, and eventually killed by a prison gang.

Both computer nerds and great hackers, Burk and Darcy were by far the best at their craft that Jeannie had ever encountered. Their combined talent helped decode a riddle found on one of Osama bin Ladin's thumb drives, revealing three separate jihadist attacks planned for the San Francisco Bay Area, one an attempt to blow up the BART tunnel running under San Francisco Bay.

"Hello, Burk," Jeannie said, hearing his voice on the phone.

"Jeannie, how are you? Darcy, it's Jeannie." Jeannie could hear Darcy in the background saying hello to her. "Hey, we miss you up here is this dysfunctional city," Burk said. "When are you coming home?"

"Soon, I hope. And that rests on you and Darcy doing your magic. I just cleared it with Flores, and I need you two to jump on my request, like yesterday."

"Let me put you on speakerphone so Darcy can hear," Burk interrupted.

"What do you need Jeannie?" asked Darcy.

Pictures of Noe Munoz were massed produced and issued to every patrol officer at their daily briefings. Additionally, the officers were instructed to visit every bar, diner and casino where Munoz's picture was displayed. A detective armed with a search warrant went to the casino where James worked and found that the video surveillance tapes showing Munoz were still available. Jeannie felt that the noose around Lobo's neck was tightening; however, by early that evening he had not been sighted. Another day came to an end. *Will he strike tonight?* Jeannie asked herself on the dreaded drive home to Newark.

Before she could get out of her bureau Crown Vic, Delores was at the driver's door. "Hi Jeannie. Did the information I gave you the other night help you solve the case yet?" she asked excitedly.

"We're getting close," Jeannie replied, noticing a stack of legal-sized documents in Delores's right hand.

Noticing Jeannie attention to them, Delores said, "Oh, I'm going around the neighborhood trying to get signatures for a petition to make it a federal law that ballots can only be cast in person and with legal identification required. Did you know that for over 200 years, all ballots had to be casted in person on the day of the election--not before or after? This crap about mail-in ballots is ripe for fraud. Even old President Carter said so back in his day. Is it asking too much of a voter to get off their behind and actually go to a polling place and cast their ballot? Think about how you could reduce fraud. You go to your poll place, show your ID, go into a booth, cast your ballot, and then you place it in a locked box."

She finally came up for air, and Jeannie, who agreed with the concept, reached for the petition and signed it. "Oh, thank you so much. Well, I have a lot of houses to hit. Let me know when we solve the case," Delores said, emphasizing the "we."

Jeannie entered the house, placed her purse and gun on the kitchen counter, and greeted her fish while dropping food pellets into their tank. She hoped to start training them to eat out of her hand soon, providing she could find her little stool that would comfortably elevate her reach over the top of the aquarium. She used to love it when her girlfriends came over to watch her father feed his koi collection in their large inground pond in the backyard. The girls were at first frightened as the koi came up from the bottom of the pond and slurped the food, gliding over one other in an eating frenzy. She knew that someday she would probably have to hire someone to install a pond in her backyard, because in about a year her current koi would have outgrown their indoor tank and would have to be replaced by younger, smaller ones.

After a light dinner and while cleaning up the dishes, Jeannie's phone rang. *God! I hope that son-of-a-bitch hasn't killed someone else,* she thought. She checked the phone display and saw it was Burk. "Hi Burk, tell me you have something good to share."

"Actually, we have a lot! Let me put you on speakerphone so Darcy can join in."

"Hi Jeannie," Darcy said. "I hope you have a pen and notepad in front of you. This is one sick puppy."

Jeannie quickly ran upstairs to her middle bedroom for a notepad and pen. "Fire away."

Burk started with basic background information. "Noe Munoz, born in Mexico City on October thirty-first, nineteen eighty-nine, which was Halloween in the U.S., and Day of the Dead in Mexico. Well, actually, Mexico celebrates Day of the Dead on both November first and second, but I digress. As you already know, he has a California driver's license and a dirt bike registered to him. It turns out that the registration address is nothing more than a P.O Box, no longer used. Darcy, however, has the juicy stuff."

"OK Jeannie, here goes," Darcy said. Jeannie could hear her shuffling papers in her hands. "His mother and father were killed when he was twelve years old. But get this, the police suspected, but couldn't prove, that he set their home on fire. Neighbors interviewed after the fire said that his father used to beat him unmercifully. No forensic work was done on the corpses, so it's pure speculation that he was involved.

"He moved in with his grandparents, but constantly got into trouble at school. He was suspended several times for fighting and stealing stuff from his fellow classmates, and also got caught with a jar containing animal parts, but he claimed he found them on his way to school. One arrest record showed that he got caught dissecting chickens he stole from a neighbor. The last straw was when he struck a male teacher and they found he had a knife. This resulted in expulsion, and he was subsequently sent to their version of a juveniles prison.

"Now here's the interesting part. After doing time, he got a job working at a ski resort at a place called Pico De Orizaba, the highest mountain in Mexico--over eighteen-thousand feet high. There's actually a glacier at the top of the mountain. It attracts some of the most elite mountain climbers in the world. Fortunately, we found employees there that still remember Munoz and say he was strange, but super a talented mountain climber who could have become one of their best instructors or guides."

"What happened?" Jeannie asked.

"Again, they all said he was just strange. He'd make bizarre comments, and was accused several times of inappropriately touching females. He was terminated after getting caught stealing guests' valuables from dressing rooms. It wouldn't take a big leap to conclude that this is where he got that ice axe. Following his termination, he paid a coyote and entered Texas illegally, finally arriving in San Jose where he lived with his aunt. She died early last year, so he's been on his own since then."

"God, please tell me! How did you two get hold of those reports?" Jeannie asked.

"You want to tell her, Burky?" Darcy asked, laughing.

"I'd love to. Yes, Jeannie, I have all of the reports in my hot hands, and man you're not going to believe what's in them. This includes the psych evaluations from when he was in prison."

"Just give the highlights and fax me the entire report afterward," Jeannie said. "I'll text the fax number to you once I get to the police department. Go ahead Burk."

"This guy's father was a sick bastard. He was a drunk, and when he wasn't beating the hell out of Noe's mom, he targeted Munoz. The father not only beat and sexual abused him, but for discipline he'd chain Noe to a post and place his food and water just out of reach, where the chain wouldn't let him go. He'd leave him there for hours in the hot Mexican sun."

"Jesus," Jeannie said. "This all coincides with the psychological profile I made up. I talked to a burned-out teacher several years ago, and he said he was considering writing a novel titled, It's the Parents Stupid, since he saw a direct correlation between students with oppositional defiant disorders and their dysfunctional parents and homelives. Part of me pities Munoz. He was doomed from the start. I hope his father is burning in hell. Does he have any living relatives?"

"I'm glad you asked," Darcy said. "The answer is no, but we checked and found that the aunt he was living with also died in a fire, a trailer in this case. The police suspected arson when his aunt's home burned, but when they tried to locate Noe, he wasn't anywhere to be found, so the case is still open."

CHAPTER TWENTY-SIX

Tuesday morning, an Uber driver dropped Anita Bryant off at the San Francisco Police Headquarters located at 1245 3rd Street. Finally taking her friend's advice, Anita decided to turn in her boyfriend, Jerome, for the vicious assaults she had repeatedly endured at his hands. Still badly bruised with a swollen left eye and cut lower lip, she was escorted to the desk of Detective Carol Anderson, an 18-year investigator specializing in female assaults. Anita had already told part of her story to desk sergeant Linda Ornellas, but Detective Anderson required a more detail report.

She began to detail her ordeal. "On Saturday night I went to see my boyfriend, Jerome, at his apartment. Out of nowhere he went into a rage and slapped me so hard I stumbled and hit my head on the wall, then he slugged me and knocked me to the ground. He grabbed me by the hair and dragged me to a couch, jumped on top of me, and continued to hit and slap me. He's so strong I couldn't roll off the couch and leave. I lost consciousness and when I woke up, still on the couch, he had taken all my clothes off. Everything was a haze and I found blood from needle marks on both arms and breasts. I have no idea what he shot into me. I could see him out of the corner of my eye and waited until he went into the bedroom. I guess he thought I was still out of it, and that's when I escaped."

Detective Anderson got the needed information about Jerome's complete name and address, type of car he drove, and issued an APB (all-points bulletin) for his arrest for attempted murder.

Two San Jose Police detectives went to the hospital with a photo line for Mrs. Lamott. She was shown a file displaying eight photos of similarly looking individuals. She looked at the top row and started on the second, then immediately said, "That's him, pointing to a picture of Noe Munoz. That's the person who killed by poor husband," she said and started to cry. One of the two detectives called Jeannie and told her they had a positive identification.

"It's coming together," she said to Farnsworth's secretary as she passed by, attempting to track him down and share the good news.

At the Story Road Home Depot, undercover narcotic officers Erik Larson and Jimmy Ng were interviewing landscaping contractor Nick Laird. "Sure, I know

Lobo," he told the officers after looking at a copy of Noe's driver's license. "He's one strange dude I can tell you, and not very reliable. Here's someone who might be able to give you more information," he said, nodding at a 30+ year-old Latino male. "Hey, Juan. You got a minute?" Juan suspiciously approached, recognizing the two men with Laird were police.

"Juan, we're not here to hassle you. I'm sergeant Larson and this is my partner officer Ng. Do you know this individual?" he asked, showing him Lobo's driver's license photo. Juan looked at it and said, "Si, Lobo. He's loco en la cabeza."

"When did you see him last?" Officer Ng asked.

"Oh, maybe a few weeks ago. He worked with me and my compadres at Mr. Shanahan's orchard and I think a few others."

"Why do you say he was crazy?" Larson asked.

"The stories he told," he responded, making the sign of the cross. "He liked to talk about the animals he tortured and then cut up. He said he killed a neighbor's cat in Mexico and cut it up in pieces. Then for fun, he put the head on the neighbor's porch with the two paws next to the head, so it looked like the cat was looking up at whoever opened the front door. He's sick man."

Ng asked what type of worker Munoz was? "When he worked, he was good. But then he would disappear, just walk away from the trees. Mrs. Shanahan caught him looking into the windows of their house once.

He told us that when the bitch caught him, he told her he was looking for the *bano*.

"Do you know where he lives?" Ng asked.

"No, he has no house. He lives with the homeless over there by the freeway."

"What freeway?" Ng asked.

"On the side of the six-eighty freeway by Berryessa." Juan answered, and continued. "At least that's the last I heard. He drove an old dirt bike that smoked like hell. I don't know what kind." Sgt. Larson called the information in to Jeannie, who in turn passed it on to Farnsworth.

"Girl, why didn't you tell the police what you think that piece of shit Jerome is doing with that white boy?" Shannel asked after learning that Anita had gone to the SFPD. She pleaded with Anita to return and tell the officer the real reason Jerome had beaten her. "If I do that, and he finds out, he'll kill me for sure." Anita finally caved, and the two drove back to the police department in Shannel's car.

Detective Anderson who had previously interviewed Anita, greeted the two when they were escorted to her desk. Anita knew there was no going back. If Jerome or Justin found out she had cooperated with the police, she would be dead. Reluctantly, she told Anderson what she knew.

Anita told her that on the night of the beating she entered Jerome's apartment and found him using pliers, attempting to remove his braces. She said that earlier she had seen the sketch on television of a person being sought for killing some police officers. Anderson abruptly stopped the interview, and excusing herself, picked up the phone and called the homicide division. "Hey, you need to come down here. I have a witness with information on your case."

Homicide Captain Sam Walters met Detective Anderson in the hallway as she was walking with Anita and Shannel to a private interview room. "What do you have?" he asked.

"We might have one-half of the cop killing team," she whispered so that neither Anita nor Shannel couldn't hear.

"You shitting me?" he asked. Anderson did not respond. She opened the door to the private interview room, introducing Captain Walters in the process.

Walters saw the physical trauma to Anita's face and was already surmising where this was going. "Would you mind starting from the beginning again, Anita?"

Anita paused, looked at Walters and Anderson, and after Shannel took her hands, she started her story again. "I saw that picture you all have been putting on the television of the guy who shot the police officer. It looked like Jerome, but hell, it could be anyone. I went to his apartment and found the front door open, so I walked in and heard him in the bathroom. When I got close, I could see that he was using a pair of pliers, trying to remove his braces. When I asked what he was going, he screamed at me and told me to mind my own business. He then told me the cops had arrested the wrong person for the donut shop shooting and admitted he had done it. He said that he and Justin had a game going on to see who could kill the most pigs. I'm sorry, but that's the word he used."

"Go on," said Anderson.

"Justine was Jerome's cell mate at Folsom prison, and that's where they became friends." "Do you know Justine's last name?" Captain Walters asked.

"I don't know his last name. He's a white boy. Actually, they grew up in the same neighborhood but didn't become close until they started doing time together." Walters knew the information he was getting was the break that law enforcement was hoping for. He would call Ismail Flores at the FBI once they wrapped up the interview.

CHAPTER TWENTY-SEVEN

"Hey man, that was cool. That Nazi never knew what hit him," Jerry Austin said to his friend Sam Welch as they watched a scene from The Great Escape, the movie where Steve McQueen stretched a wire across a country road, knocking off a German soldier driving a motorcycle with a side car.

"Yeah," said Welch. "We should try that in the school parking lot sometime. That would really screw up someone's day. Maybe we could knock off our quarterback Jimmy Ratcliff when he enters the student parking lot. I'd pay to see that."

Welch and Austin lived in San Jose's Story and King area, not the greatest area of the city. Both had been expelled the week before for starting trash receptacle fires in two of the high school girl's bathrooms. Incorrigible was not a strong enough adjective to describe them. Both lived with single mothers who cared more about themselves than carrying out their parental responsibilities. In fact, when either of the two got in trouble, the mothers would try to turn the table and accuse the authorities of harassment.

Both kids were failing in school, but in liberal California no child was held back a grade level. Instead, in fear of hurting a student's self-esteem, teachers just pushed the proverbial can down the road until these forgotten students ended up failing to graduate from high school. By then, social labeling had taken place, coupled with name calling and bullying. Cutting school and getting high was their only goal.

Between the two, Sam was the leader. He had already served numerous times in the county's juvenile hall and the judge told him that one more offense would land him in the California Youth Authority, a prison for minors. Sam's dad was already doing time in Soledad Prison, so he was just following in his father's footsteps. His mother had a medical marijuana prescription which she shared with her son. She was currently holding down two jobs to survive and was only at home to sleep, shower, and return to work. For the most part, Sam had the house to himself and could to do whatever he wished during his mother's frequent absences.

Jerry's dad died of a heroin overdose when he was eight-years old. His mom brought a string of males into their house to satisfy her sexual needs. One of them tried to rape his sister, and Jerry stabbed him in the back with a butcher's knife. The wound was not serious and the male fled the residence, never to return. No one pressed charges. The mother was collecting welfare and still had a little of her father's life insurance money put away, but the family pretty much survived as Sam's family did.

Turning off the television, Sam made sure his bedroom door was locked and pulled out a binder from between his mattress and box springs. He opened it and unfolded a crude map showing the layout of their high school. Jerry looked at it and said, "If we pull this off, everyone will forget about Columbine."

"Yeah, but we won't be like those lame asses that did Columbine," Jerry said. If we do this right, we can take out a lot more people before they get us. I'm thinking that we put some more pipe bombs in this area (pointing to the map), but we don't set them off during our initial assault. We wire them to go off after we know the cops are in those areas. I heard on the news that this was a tactic ISIS was using in the Middle East. They would set off a bomb and draw the army units to the area to rescue the injured. That's when they'd activate the bigger IUD, taking out even more people. What do you think?"

"Sounds good, " Sam said. "But we'll need some kind of trigger devices we can activate with our cellphones. Also, we'll have to install a few cameras we can monitor so we'll know when to set off these secondary devices. Let's do a quick weapons check and then decide what other equipment we'll need.

Soon, those asshole motherfuckers at school will get what they deserve."

The briefing room was packed to the rafters. Bottled water, soda and cookies were spread out on a table near the back wall. Jeannie was surprised that she still had a lot of energy after several unrestful nights. She and Farnsworth were both leaning on a table at the front of the crowd.

Approaching the microphone, Farnsworth began speaking. "OK, people. Grab a seat." He had opened his binder and Jeannie could see a paper listing action items to discuss. "I've broken you into teams. Some of you have been assigned to various sectors of the county's freeway system. I don't have to tell you that the number of homeless encampments along these roadways are growing. We chase them out, and they set up somewhere else. Our latest information is that the suspect lives somewhere in these encampments.

"Others have been assigned, along with patrol and the Santa Clara County Sheriff's Department, to saturate county segments having orchards, ranches, and farms. Today marks the sixth day since his last kill. He's due for another. Using caution, we need to root him out of there and take him into custody. We have no indication he's got a gun, but assume he does. He's…sorry Jeannie, no offense, but knowing that psychologists don't like this term I'm going to say it anyway…he's crazy."

The room filled with laughter as Jeannie threw up her hands with a huge smile on her face and said, "None taken." Farnsworth released the group.

Munoz felt something bite his forehead and smashed a blood filled mosquito with his hand. Feeling hungry, he slipped out of his sleeping bag and stretched. Although a full moon, the heavy shrubs bordering the freeway blocked most if it's reflected light. Some in the encampment were still awake and keeping warm by small campfires. He reached into the bag and pulled out his tool, massaging the pointed end and smiling. Obeying his urge, he headed for his motorcycle, kicked the kickstand and started to insert the ignition key, but the kickstand had not released. Preparing to kick it again, he saw them. Fifteen feet away, two strangers who were obviously cops were talking to some of the homeless and showing them a sheet of paper.

He quickly kicked the kickstand several times, the noise alerting the officers. One of them yelled for Noe to hold up, but Noe climbed on the bike and started it, spinning dirt and gravel from the rear tire as he sped up and headed south on the freeway.

"All units. Possible suspect on motorcycle heading southbound on Highway six-eighty." Releasing the call, the two officers at the encampment joined units who were leaving their positions and moving into the target area. The California Highway Patrol helicopter quickly arrived over the encampment local, and overhearing Munoz's travel direction, made a 180 degree turn and headed south.

The new bike Munoz was driving was fast, much more so than his old dirt bike. He knew he had to get off the freeway before being spotted. If he took the next exit and crossed over highway 680, he could enter the foothills and get lost in the trees. This was the area he had planned to visit that night, so thought that he still might be able to make it to the McMichael's place. While the police searched for him, he would be dining in the McMichael's kitchen.

Sam yelled to Jerry, "Here comes one. Make sure it's tight on your end." Jerry twisted the wire around the telephone pole and tested its tautness. Satisfied, he ran across the two-lane road and slid on the dry glass next to Sam. "This will be great," he said.

Munoz gunned his high-powered motorcycle to 56 miles per hour and was preparing to pop a wheelie. The wire decapitated him instantly and his head bounced along the asphalt until it stopped rolling, lying on its side. The bike continued on its path like a headless horseman. Sam and Jerry followed the bike's aimless path for another 20 feet past Munoz's head, and after a shimmy slid on its side, sending sparks into the night sky. "Wow!" Sam said. "That was awesome!"

Jerry saw an object fall from the headless motorcycle driver and quickly ran toward it. Sirens could be heard and flashing red and blue lights could be seen in the distance. Jerry reached down and picked up the ice axe. He had little time to inspect what he had since the cops were getting close. "Let's get out of here," Sam said.

The CHP helicopter was the first to find the scene of the accident. From high above they could see the motorcycle and alerted ground units. It was not until a Sheriff's patrol unit arrived that the severed head was found. He also saw a wire stretched across the roadway. Jeannie and Farnsworth followed the progress of the pursuit from dispatch. "Let's go to the scene," Farnsworth said. Jeannie agreed.

They arrived before the coroner's office did, which was fine with Jeannie since she did not like to be hurried, especially after a long and exhausting investigation. She saw the head, but only glanced at it. Yep, that's Munoz. *Got what you deserved, dirtbag*, she thought. She was more interested in finding the ice axe.

From a standing position she could not see the left side of Munoz's body which she thought could be concealing the murder weapon. All she found was a hunting knife still in its sheath. She pulled out her trusty little flashlight and walked up and down the roadway, checking the vegetation on both sides for the axe.

"Need more light to do a proper search," she said to Farnsworth who nodded before saying they would be directing traffic around the scene until daylight, and that should help.

He looked at Munoz's head and said, "Every man is the architect of his own fortune. But for Lobo, a bad beginning makes for a bad ending. No need for us to stay here. Let me take you back to the station." Jeannie did not reply. Seeing the coroner's van arrive, she walked back to their car.

"I wonder how many more of these monsters are being created in a toxic environment by a torturous sadistic son-of-a-bitch like his father?" Jeannie asked, not expecting a reply and getting none from Farnsworth.

"Air One, this is Unit Forty-Two. We have two juveniles running from the scene. I lost them in the bushes about twenty-five feet to the west of my patrol car. Can you light up the area?"

"Roger that," came the helicopter pilot's reply, and a few minutes later added. "Got them. They're lying on the ground about ten feet from you on your left." The chopper pilot and spotter focused their strong light beam on the two juveniles being approached by the pursing officers, but before they could be apprehended, the two darted into a large drainage ditch and disappeared.

Before Lt. Farnsworth and Jeannie made it back to Highway 680, Farnsworth was asked to meet the officers at the scene. Spinning a U-turn, it did not take them long to find the officers. "Sorry sir. We thought we had them, but the two disappeared after they entered this opening," a patrol officer stated while illuminating the gapping end of a large steel pipe. "By the time we figured out where it emptied, they were gone. We followed their tracks as far as you could, but these fuckers know the area well, that's for sure."

CHAPTER TWENTY-EIGHT

It was almost 2:00 a.m. when Jeannie pulled into her driveway. *Don't have to worry about being ambushed by Delores at this hour*, she thought. She went directly to the aquarium after turning the dining room lights on. "Sorry I'm so late, guys" she said, lifting the cover and dropping in food pellets which the koi rapidly swallowed. "Yeah, I'm hungry too."

She found a Stouffer's Turkey Tetrazzini dinner in her freezer and thought it would hit the spot, not remembering the last time she had eaten. Everything came together so quickly. As she ate, she thought about everyone she needed to call the first thing in the morning. Besides giving Ismail an update, she wanted to call Lawrence and Dr. Washington and let them know that the case had been solved.

Opting for a hot shower over a bubble bath, and slipping into her robe after drying off, she visited her second bedroom and stared at the wall dedicated to the Mutilator. She started pulling off photos and documents from the whiteboard and putting them in a folder, but then realized there was no urgency in doing so and called it a day.

Upon awaking in the morning, she gave up on the idea of getting one more hour of sleep; she would take a nap later. She threw on her bathrobe, went downstairs, and started brewing a fresh pot of coffee. While waiting, she feed her koi. A fresh cup of coffee in her hand, she sat at the kitchen table and called Dr. Washington on the east coast. He eagerly digested all of the new information and the culmination of the investigation, and told Jeannie he would be the hit of that evening's Murder Club party with friends.

A little after seven o'clock and knowing that Ismail was probably getting ready to drive to the bureau, Jeannie gave him a call. He answered with, "Hey Boss lady, I was just going to give you a call. You're all over the news. Man, it's going to be hard working with you, I mean you being a celebrity and all."

"Very funny," Jeannie responded. "Nice to hear your voice too, asshole. I don't know how much detail was given to the media, but I'll fill you in later once I catch my breath and drive to the city. I hope to be there before lunch and we can get-together and focus on your case."

"I'm starting to feel better already. See you soon," he said before hanging up.

Jeannie made French toast for breakfast and drank another cup of coffee. She loved to sprinkle cinnamon on both side of the toast like her mom did. *Nothing like melted butter and warm syrup to finish off the toast,* she thought. She considered a third cup, but worried that she might run into traffic on her commute to the bureau and she did not want to have to make an emergency bathroom stop on the way.

She dressed in a light blue pants suit and gave herself one last glance in the mirror. *Shit. Looks like I added another line to my crow's feet. Oh well, still not a bad looking lady if I say so myself,* she thought. She hoped to get into her bureau car and leave the subdivision without being caught by old eagle eye Delores, but no such luck. As soon as Jeannie grabbed the driver's door handle, Delores ran from her front porch yelling Jeannie's name. "Good morning Delores," Jeannie said, stressing the point that she needed to get going by looking at her watch.

"I know you have to go, but I had to say congratulations. You even made it on Newsmax TV and One American News. Did my hunch help solve the case again?"

"Actually, Delores, it did. When you told me the story of going to your aunt's orchard to pick apricots, and that sometimes it was scary when pickers stared at you…remember?"

"Yes, yes. And how did that help?" she asked.

"Well, and this is confidential, the suspect was an extra help fruit picker." Delores covered her mouth and stared at Jeannie.

"Oh my God! You mean he used to work for those poor victims and then came back and killed them?" Jeannie did not answer; she just put her right index finger in front of her lips. Delores mimicked her action while shaking her head up and down.

Jeannie again looked at her watch in a deliberate fashion and told Delores she had to run. "Oh, OK. I'm glad I was able to help. You know, I'm getting pretty good at this stuff. Anytime you have a case that you're having a hard time solving, let me know." She then turned and began walking toward her house. Jeannie thought she saw a little skip in her steps.

The drive to the city felt good. Jeannie lowered the passenger side window a bit, allowing the smell of the salt water to invade her car as she crossed the Dumbarton Bridge. Not as good as when driving her Corvette, but not bad. Everyone she passed greeted her as she made her way from the garage to her office. She checked in with her secretary, Stephanie, who welcomed her back and then presented her with a hefty stack of "While-U-Were-Out" notes. "This will take some time to sort through," she commented.

"I tried to prioritize them," Stephanie said. "Many at the bottom came in this morning. Congratulations and so on. Oh, and this one just came in." She handed Jeannie another note from Lawrence. "He requested that you give him a call, but that it wasn't urgent."

Damn! Jeannie thought. *I should have called him right after Dr. Washington.* "Thanks Steph. Is the SAC in?"

"No, he had a dentist appointment at eleven, so I don't expect him until well after lunch," Stephanie answered.

"Hey lady, can I have an autograph?" Ismail said, coming down the hallway from the breakroom with two cups of coffee.

"Only if one of those is for me," Jeannie replied.

"Well, it can be, but most celebrities don't want to hobnob with us common folk."

"Get in here, you fool," Jeannie said to Ismail as she opened her office door. She laid the While-U-Were-Out notes on the top of her desk and reached for one the coffees.

"I sure hope you brought some of your San Jose karma back with you. So far, we still seem to be at square one," Ismail said.

Just then, Stephanie knocked on Jeannie's open office door. "Excuse me. Flo, there's an emergency call for you from a Captain Walters of the San Francisco Police Department. "There you go," said a smiling Jeannie as Ismail went down to his office to get the waiting call.

CHAPTER TWENTY-NINE

Jeannie was in the process of calling Lawrence to give him all the sorted details of the Mutilator case when Ismail raced into her office. "I'll be damned!" he said. "You do have karma. We may have just gotten our big break. Are you free to go over to the SFPD headquarters with me? I can fill you in on the way." *Sorry, Lawrence, duty calls*, Jeannie thought as she grabbed her purse and followed Ismail to the parking garage.

Ismail told Jeannie about the Jerome Mays case, and how his scorned and beaten girlfriend, Anita Bryant, had come forward. "Not the last time a woman gets even," Jeannie said.

Arriving at the SFPD headquarters, they eventually tracked down Captain Walters who took them to the second-floor breakroom. Detective Anderson was already seated when they entered. After introductions, Anderson gave a synopsis of the interview with Anita.

"Let's hope Jerome doesn't feel she's turned on him. We might be able to use that to track him down," Jeannie said. Captain Walters agreed.

Jeannie and Ismail drove back to the bureau, picking up lunch on the way, not only for them, but also Burk, Darcy, and the rest of the team. Jeannie had requested that Stephanie set everything up. *Things could break fast here like it did in San Jose,* she thought. *So, who knows when they might get a chance to eat?*

As soon as lunch was over and duties were assigned, Burk and Darcy began a workup on Jerome Mays. They had hoped that in the process they might come up with additional information on Justin. They got into the standard data bases, DMV and NCIC, including some sites Jeannie did not want to know about.

Two hours later Darcy called Jeannie. "This guy, Jerome, is no stranger to crime. He has an extensive juvenile record including grand theft auto, residential burglary, arson, and attempted rape. A liquor store robbery netted a six-year stay in Folsom. There's a parole hold out for him for failure to report. The last known address is the one Anita gave the SFPD, but they haven't seen any activity there. The DMV didn't have any vehicles registered to him. Sorry, we couldn't find anything on Justine, but we have a call into the warden at Folsom."

Burk came on the line. "Jeannie, Darcy and I are going to take a break and visit some high schools located in the area that Anita said were his old haunts. Maybe we'll luck out."

"Sounds good. Keep me posted," Ismail said.

Ismail knocked on Jeannie's open office door, waving a search warrant for Jerome's apartment. "SFPD had the place under surveillance until they turned it over to our team, but so far there hasn't been any activity." Jeannie's phone rang. It was SAC Lomax. "How was the dentist?" she asked.

"I don't want to talk about it," he grumbled. "Congratulations on the Mutilator case. Farnsworth sent an Atta-Girl to the Director in Washington. You should be getting a copy soon. I heard from Stephanie that you finally got a break. I won't be in until tomorrow morning and we can touch bases then. Two root canals can spoil your day!"

Walking to the garage, Jeannie stopped abruptly and said to Ismail, "I owe you an apology. This is your case and I came in here like a bull in a China shop and took over. I'll back off. It's your show."

"Are you kidding me? What would Batman be without Robin, or Abbott without Costello, or Laurel without Hardy, and let's not forget the Lone Ranger and Tonto? As Forrest Gump said, you and me are like peas and carrots. Now let's go and hunt this bastard down," Ismail said.

They arrived at Jerome's apartment. Fortunately, it was an end unit, and if they were quiet, maybe the neighbors would not notice. It was a tense moment since they did not know for certain whether Jerome was inside. Jeannie had two SWAT members open the door using the key provided by the apartment manager. The apartment was clear.

Survivalist magazines and weapon manuals were scattered everywhere. They found a guide for terrorist operations and how to conduct surveillance. Another publication outlined how to conceal one's movements and how to catch a victim by surprise. A nightstand drawer held nude pictures of Anita as well as a diary. The diary contained anti-police rhetoric interspersed with hand-drawn pictures of police officers sporting bull's eyes on their bodies.

Nearly finished with the search, Ismail looked between the bed mattresses and found a black ski mask similar to the one a witness saw Jerome discard following the liquor store shooting. He also found 9mm cartridges wrapped in a plastic bag and a Ingram MAC 10 users' manual he showed to Jeannie. "Starting to come together," he said, as he confiscated the items.

Jeannie ordered the 24-hour surveillance to continue, just in case Jerome returned. "I'll try to find a conservative deputy DA and get a wiretap on both Anita's cell and Jerome's, but if he knows he's hot, he's probably already ditched it," she told Ismail.

Agent Parson was assigned the job of showing a photo spread to the taxi driver who got the best view of the killer when the culprit hailed a cab, fleeing the scene. The cabbie wasted no time positively identifying Jerome as the shooter. A rushed hair analysis was requested for the hair found in the ski cap Ismail found in Jerome's apartment and the hair clinging to the cap Jerome discarded in the alley. By evening, Jeannie was notified of a match. "You're right Ace," she said. "It's coming together."

CHAPTER THIRTY

Finding another conservative deputy DA, they presented all the evidence they had on Jerome Mays. Two witnesses, Anita and the cabbie, positively identified and implicated him in the killing of at least two officers. The third witness was science itself--the hair sample analysis. Without hesitation, the DA issued an arrest warrant on Jerome Mays for multiple homicides. Now, all they had to do was find him. Jeannie took a calculated risk and did not put the warrant into the NCIC computer system, hoping that Jerome would either lead them to Justin or stop by to visit the apartment.

Two days passed and there was still no sight of Jerome or the mysterious Justin. Jeannie contemplated calling off the surveillance, feeling that Jerome had fled the area; but fortunately, she did not. That afternoon the surveillance team advised that a blonde male walked up to the apartment and knocked on the door. Jeannie ordered them to detain the subject until she and Ismail arrived.

As the surveillance team approached the blonde male, and before the team members could identify themselves, Justin began to run, a handgun falling from his waistband in the process. He did not stop to retrieve it. One of the two officers who ran marathons for a hobby had no problem catching up to Justin and bringing him down with a tackle. His wallet showed a driver's license for Justin Peterson, 32 years old, with an address in the Haight district. An SFPD patrol car arrived and Justin was placed in the backseat where he remained until Ismail and Jeannie arrived. Following a custody transfer, Justin found himself cuffed to the center of a table at the cities' FBI headquarters. Jeannie and Ismail tried several ploys to get Justine to talk, but he refused--only repetitiously demanding his lawyer.

Legal concluded they had enough evidence on Justin to issue a search warrant on his apartment. The Haight District of San Francisco bordering Golden Gate Park was the birthplace of the 1960's counterculture. Justin's apartment was located on Upper Haight Street which consists of a hodgepodge of vintage clothing boutiques, record and CD shops, bookstores, dive bars and casual, eclectic restaurants. One does not have to look hard to find the Hippie Movement imprint.

Jeannie requested that the SFPD supply at least two of their uniformed officers to assist when they entered the apartment. The apartment was typical for this section of San Francisco, and perhaps for most of the city. It was a half of what was once a large apartment located on the third floor. A non-bearing wall now divided the floor into two separate units. A knock on the door failed to elicit a response. Not finding an available landlord, Jeannie pulled out the trusty lockpick set her father gave her and went to work. *Not much of a challenge*, she thought as the lock easily released from its receiver.

Like most of the Haight, the apartment reeked of marijuana. Justine had eight plants growing near his kitchen. "Medicinal use," Ismail said. Jeannie just smiled.

"I'll take this bedroom and the kitchen, you take the second bedroom and the bath. We can check the front room last," Jeannie said as she headed to the self-assigned bedroom. Ismail found survivalist magazines and upcoming gun show brochures lying around the apartment, subject matter similar to other materials strewn about. Black shooting silhouettes covered one wall, but Justine had placed a police badge over the heart area of each one.

"Cute," Ismail said out loud to himself.

Then he heard Jeannie yell, "Bingo!"

"What do you have, boss?" Ismail asked as he entered the bedroom Jeannie was searching. She had several photos of Officer Roy Graham, his wife and twin daughters coming and going from their home, all spread out on the bed. "This bastard was surveilling them before he killed Graham," Ismail said. "If the gun that fell from his waistband is a match to that killing, he's toast."

Jeannie pulled out her phone and called Stephanie, requesting that she send their forensic crime scene team for evidence collection. Ending the call, she said to Ismail, "I'll have them dust for prints here, just like Jerome's apartment. It'll be helpful to have prints showing that they had been in each other's abodes. Did I tell you that Burk and Darcy didn't find any mutual emails on either of their computers? Only crap from survivalist's sites and firearms. They seem to have been knowledgeable enough to hide their correspondence."

"If we get prints, it's frosting on the cake," Ismail replied.

A month passed without any Jerome sightings. He had gone underground. The more brainstorming Jeannie and her team did, the more frustrated everyone became. Would he kill another officer? Had he moved to another state? Police agencies throughout Northern California continued their search in a state of urgency and desire for revenge. Numerous sightings were received, but none panned out. *No, Jerome disappeared for parts unknown, or had he*? Jeannie mused to herself.

Having reported to SAC Lomax that once again they had not made progress in the investigation, Jeannie called it a day. As she told a depressed Ismail when there were no breaks in his case, she needed to be patient. She picking up Chinese food on the trip home and ate it upstairs in her second bedroom, staring at the wall dedicated to the cop killers' case versus the Mutilator. *How do I draw you out, you son-of-a-bitch? Maybe I should consult with Delores*? she thought, the Delores consultation idea causing her to laugh and lightly choke on Chinese noodles.

CHAPTER THIRTY-ONE

The next morning, she left the bureau car at home and drove her Corvette into the city. With open windows, she set her heater on max to compensate for the cold brisk sea air coming off the water under Dumbarton Bridge. Hoping for inspiration, she turned on her favorite conservative radio talk show and unsuccessfully tried to get the case out of her mind.

Jeannie found the topic being discussed an interesting one: Are Men Angrier Than Women? "Sure, men are," she said out loud to her radio. The guest female psychologist reported that most people surveyed on the topic believe men get angrier more often than women, and that males are more short-tempered than females. Females are perceived as more tolerant and peace-loving. "There you go," Jeannie agreed out loud.

The guest speaker went on to say that the "majority view" suggests that women's anger displays are often labeled unladylike or worse, while anger displays in men are rationalized as powerful or dominant. "Just like that song by Blue Stream, Big Boys Don't Cry," Jeannie said as she began to sing some of the lyrics.

The psychologist went on to say that in the overwhelming majority of surveys and studies conducted to date, it has been found that men and women get angry just as often and just as intensely as one another, and seek anger management counseling in roughly equal numbers. Few studies have found women angrier than men. "Huh, learned something already today," Jeannie said to herself. It was at that point, midspan on the Dumbarton Bridge, that Jeannie's proverbial light bulb came on. "I have an idea on how to draw you out, asshole!" she exclaimed to the passing wind.

When Jeannie arrived at the bureau and before she could tell Ismail her plan, Stephanie said that Captain Walters of the SFPD had just called and left a message that Anita had received a phone message from Jerome asking her to call him. "My plan is going to work," Jeannie responded, receiving a quizzical look from her receptionist. She found Burk, Darcy and Ismail in the breakroom. Having said good morning to everyone, she shared her plan, feeling confident it would work, particularly since Jerome had reached out to Anita.

"What? He did? When?" came from Darcy. "I'd thought he'd be long gone by now."

Jeannie poured herself a cup of coffee and sat down with the group, allowing them to process her plan to utilize Anita. Following the meeting, Jeannie and Ismail drove to Anita's safehouse, one that the bureau had set up for her. They called her before arriving, requesting that she accompany them to the bureau where they would outline their plan to locate Jerome.

At the bureau, Anita was seated in a small soundproof room with Jeannie and Ismail. Darcy and Burk were in their office, having already set up monitoring equipment in an effort to triangulate Jerome's cell once Anita placed a phone call. Jeannie hoped that Jerome would not suspect them of listening in. As Anita made the call, Darcy and Burk tracked the ping to the 400 block of Oyster Point Boulevard in South San Francisco. Units were dispatched to the area, but Jerome was not there. The cellphone had been deactivated. "Shit!" Jeannie said when Darcy notified her.

The next morning, Jeannie received a call from Ismail. "Anita got another call from Jerome, and he gave her a new phone number. It's probably a burner--but get this, he says he's heading to Arizona. She asked him where he was--you know, his current location--but he wouldn't tell her. If you remember, Anita told us that when they were together he constantly monitored the police, so he's probably doing the same now. He has to know by now that he's hot."

"So, the prick may or may not be driving to Arizona in an unknown model or type of car. Can't do much with that, can we? Plus, we don't know if Jerome suspects Anita's working with the cops, but we have to assume he does. We need to draw him back to this area, and I think I know a way," Jeannie said.

Anita was brought back to the bureau and situated in the small soundproof room again with Ismail while Jeannie met with the SAC. "Jeannie, you know your neck and mine are way out there by deliberately withholding Jerome's arrest warrant in the system. So far, we've done a pretty good job keeping his name out of the media, but you know that secrets are hard to keep--even in law enforcement."

"Believe me, I've lost a lot of sleep these last few days worrying about that," Jeannie said. "But if he finds out he's wanted, he may go underground and we'll never find him. Plus, my idea for luring him out will only work if he feels he might still be in the clear. Or, if his motive is more sinister…"

"More sinister. You mean he wants to kill Anita?" Lomax asked. Jeannie nodded in response.

"Don't get me wrong, Jeannie. We know we're between a rock and a hard place, but I don't think there's any other way to play this. To catch him, we need to keep his name out of the media and surprise him. That also means keeping his arrest warrant out of the national system. It's a risk we have to take, but he could be stalking an officer right now. Please, keep me in the loop."

Outside Fresno on Highway 5, CHP (California Highway Patrol) Officer Jim Maxwell, three weeks from retirement, activated his emergency equipment and pulled Jerome over for speeding. "Can I see your driver's license and registration, please?" Officer Maxwell asked. Jerome gave Maxwell the car's registration, but claimed his driver's license was in the trunk. Maxwell had Jerome walk to the rear of the vehicle were Jerome opened the trunk. Watching him closely, Maxwell saw Jerome rifle through his belongings and pull out his license. He handed it to Officer Maxwell who told him to return to the vehicle.

Maxwell requested a wants and warrants check. The car had not been reported as stolen and was legally registered to a rental company. Maxwell walked to the driver's side of the vehicle and had Jerome sign a citation for excessive speed, and released him. The opportunity to catch the cop killer was missed.

On a leisure early Saturday morning, Jeannie, still in her nightwear, brought her breakfast into the dining room, hoping her fish might provide insight into another avenue of pursuit. "Got any ideas, guys and gals, because I have zilch?" She noticed that two of her male koi's were chasing one of the females around the tank. "Knock it off," she said. "That could be construed as sexual harassment." She picked up her plate and was walking back to the kitchen when she was hit by a thought: *That's it! That's how to get him to surface*!

She called Ismail, but got his wife instead. "Hi Jeannie. Boy you're up early."

"Hi. Yes, I couldn't sleep after six. You're going to kill me, but I need to pick Ismail up and take him to the city with me."

"Hey, the way he's moping around the house, I'd love for you to get him out of here. Let me get him for you. Izzy, its Jeannie on the phone for you."

Jeannie picked up Ismail forty-five minutes later. "I have an idea and I need to put it in play immediately. We can't wait for this prick to kill another officer. Call Anita and tell her to be ready in about an hour. We'll stop at the bureau so I can pick up my Crown Vic, and I'll drop you off. You, Burk, and Darcy get all of the monitoring equipment ready so that when I return with her, we can make the call.

"What's your plan boss, or do you want me to guess?" Ismail asked, turning to Jeannie.

"Look, we both know that Jerome's unstable and actively killing cops. We have to create a reason for him to return to the bay area. At this stage we're at his mercy--he's calling the shots. We need to get him nailed down in one location and surround him, and we need to rely on Anita again. That's the only constant. I need her to make another phone call to him, and I hope the phone number is still good. If it's not, I can coach her on what to say if he calls."

CHAPTER THIRTY-TWO

Anita was ready when Jeannie knocked on her door. They discussed the plan on the ride back to the bureau. "I want you to tell him that you want to reconcile, and then while he's thinking about it, tell him you're pregnant with his child."

The last cell phone number given to Anita rang four times, and Jeannie began to think it had already been tossed; but on the fifth ring, Jerome answered. Jerome seemed interested, but would not say where or when they would meet again. Jeannie worried that they might be losing the element of surprise. He said he would call her the next day and then hung up.

Jeannie felt they needed a bit of edge, so she told Anita that when he called back to say that she knows the sex of the baby and to ask Jerome if he wants a boy or a girl. After stating his preference, say that she had an exam, and that his preference is the sex of the fetus. It doesn't matter what sex he wants, just go with it.

That afternoon, they lost their edge. Somehow the media found out about the case and began broadcasting Jerome's name and photograph. This brought the entire investigation to a heightened level. She hoped Jerome had not seen the broadcast, but it was all over social media.

Memorial Day weekend arrived. Jerome had not returned Anita's call for four days. Jeannie and her team worried that he saw the news and was long gone; but then he called, telling Anita he was ready to meet with her. Hoping he would eventually call, Jeannie had instructed Anita to request a meeting at the San Francisco Zoo located in the southwestern corner of San Francisco, between Lake Merced and the Pacific Ocean along the Great Highway. The 100-acre zoo could easily accommodate numerous FBI agents without stirring suspicion; they could observe unnoticed.

Jerome agreed to the date, time, and location; it would be the following day. He told Anita how as a kid he used to go there to watch the monkeys on monkey island, and how sad he was that it had been removed. Jerome believed he would be meeting Anita the next morning at 11 a.m., telling her he would call once he found parking.

Jeannie had Ismail call Tim Shield, head of the bureau's SWAT unit, requesting a meet early that afternoon. Jeannie gathered her team and all the agents she would use to corral Jerome once he entered the park. Jeannie had nagging thoughts about why Jerome had decided to return to the city. He could be in love with Anita, or he realized that killing her would remove a witness to his crimes. Maybe he returned because he wanted to kill another cop, or both. She couldn't allow either to happen.

SFPD undercover officers as well as FBI agents saturated the zoo. Since he had mentioned the old monkey island exhibit, Jeannie instructed Anita to tell Jerome she would be waiting in that same area, near the bird aviary depicting South America. Jeannie and Ismail would set up there. Jeannie was wearing a pair of distressed jeans and a flannel shirt, her hair in a ponytail. She decided against wearing a baseball cap after looking at herself in the mirror before leaving home. She felt it made her look too much like a cop.

Ismail sat across from Jeannie on another bench about 40 feet away, wearing a pair of runner's sweatpants and a 49ers jacket with fake leather sleeves that looked like a varsity jacket. They waited, ready for action. Burk and Darcy were at the bureau in a room with Anita, waiting for Jerome's phone call.

Jeannie continued to second guess herself as to whether she had everything covered. A perimeter had been set up--check. Once Jerome was seen entering the zoo, units would track his movement--check. All possible escape routes were covered--check. All officers reported they were in position--check. SWAT was standing by and everyone's radio traffic was silenced;

no one shared any levity. The silence could be cut with a knife. Waiting was the worst part.

"All units," Burk announced. "The subject just called and is trying to find a parking space at the main entrance." Jeannie was still second guessing herself. This should be a routine operation. Many people feel these situations are the most hazardous for law enforcement, but in reality, calls to domestic cases and vehicle stop are more dangerous.

Jeannie switched channels on her radio so that she would be talking only with Ismail. "You know Ace, he won't go peacefully."

"Well, if we have to take him down hard, we'll be saving taxpayers a lot of money," Ismail replied.

Jerome called. He wanted to change the meeting location to a site fifteen miles away. Jeannie warned Anita during coaching that this might happen. "Jerome, I can't just get up and meet you. I need to be by a bathroom. I'm not feeling well during these early stages of pregnancy and I won't do anything to hurt our baby. Now, if you want to see me and say hi to our unborn child, you best get over here. It's so nice inside, and warm. Come on, I know you like alligators and crocodiles, or whatever they are. There's even supposed to be a big anaconda in here."

"OK. I'm on my way. You said it's by the old monkey island location?"

"Yes, see you soon." This new information was passed on to all units. "Do you think he knows he's being set up?" Jeannie asked Ismail.

"We'll soon find out," Ismail answered. *Will he change his mind and leave?* Jeannie wondered. Once again, Jerome seemed to be calling the shots. Jeannie had another terrible thought run through her head. What if Jerome just wanted to get into shooting range of Anita since she was the only witness who could place him at the shooting. He had forgotten about the cabbie. Pressure continued to mount.

Darcy notified all units that Jerome had called Anita again, and that he was heading toward the old monkey island location. "Why did you have to go so far inside the zoo?" Jeremy asked Anita upon seeing her.

"Jerome, have you ever been pregnant? I don't think so. You'll see how nice and warm it is inside, and I love the sound of the waterfall. Besides, I'm right by a bathroom, and boy am I using it. Now get your black ass in here."

"All units, this is unit one. I have a visual on the subject. He just entered the park."

"Unit three sees him now. He's walking quickly toward the aviary. He's glancing all around him--a little hinky. He's wearing a black bomber-style jacket and blue jeans. No hat."

A few minutes passed with no updates. Jeannie started to panic. "Unit four, do you have him?" she asked.

"Negative. He must've turned right and will probably approach the meeting area from the southside."

"Unit five. He just rounded the corner and is still walking toward the aviary."

"Roger that. Ismail, get ready. He should be coming in the door straight ahead of you, behind my back. Let him approach until he's past me, then we take him down. Don't get in my crossfire," Jeannie said.

"Not a problem," Ismail replied. He saw Jerome reach for the entrance door to the aviary, then stop. "Something must have spooked him," Ismail said to Jeannie. Jerome turned and began to slowly jog, retracing his path to the aviary. He quickly pulled out a handgun from his waistband and fired at a male sitting on a bench reading a magazine, minding his own business.

Jeannie and Ismail arrived at the entrance door at the same time, both seeing Jerome run toward the heavy foliage lining the pathway. He hung a left and jumped into the bushes for cover. Jeannie was right; he was going to go down hard.

FBI agent Lawrence, hearing Jeannie's directions, entered the jungle-like plants and bushes area only to immediately come face-to-face with Jerome who fired two rounds. One round struck Lawrence in the forehead. Now in panic mode, Jerome discarded his jacket and pulled his shirt over his head, turning it inside out to display a different color, and then calmly put his weapon back in his waistband, but this time in the curve of his back. Exiting the shrubbery, he tried to blend in with the panic stricken and confused crowd trying to leave the zoo.

Jerome doubled back to the bird aviary and saw Anita sitting by herself. *The bitch set me up*, he thought to himself. By the time she could look up, it was too late. Jerome fired two rounds into her upper body, killing her instantly.

Jeannie and Ismail had split up, trying to get ahead and flank Jerome, but they lost track of him. Jerome, exiting the aviary, found a bare area deplete of foliage, allowing him to leave the path leading to the exit gate and get a beat on the pursuing agents. He heard the rustling of foliage, turned, and aimed his gun in that direction. They saw each other at the same time, but Jerome was the quicker of the two. He fired one round hitting Ismail on the side not protected by his bullet proof vest. Ismail's gun fell out of his hand as he fell to the ground.

Jerome began walking up to Ismail, pointing his gun to Ismail's head.

"Hello Jerome," Jeannie said as she fired three rounds into his chest. Jerome had a surprised look on his face as he looked at his shirt which was quickly becoming saturated with his own blood. He looked at Jeannie who fired a fourth round into his forehead. Dropping his gun, Jerome fell to the ground face first. She saw that Ismail was still conscious. "Hang in there, Ace," she said as she knelled down by him.

"Not going anywhere, boss." Turning his gaze to Jerome's body he added, "By the way, the taxpayers of California thank you."

CHAPTER THIRTY-THREE

No matter how hard she tried, Jeannie could not sleep in on Saturday morning. *Too much adrenaline,* she thought. She decided to make it a productive day and maybe take a nap later. Her whole house was in need of a clean-up, especially her second bedroom now that the Mutilator case was closed. Making her way to the kitchen, she splurged and made French toast and sausage for breakfast.

Ricky, her deceased fiancé, would be proud of her. When they lived together he used to scold her when she wanted to skip breakfast. "It's the most important meal of the day," she could still hear him say. She felt a tear coming on and brushing it away, grabbed her first morning cup of coffee.

She took her breakfast to the dining room and set the plate on the table. Before eating, she opened the top of her aquarium and dropped a few pellets into the tank and waiting mouths of her hungry koi. "Good morning guys and gals. We have a busy day planned," she told them.

Having finishing breakfast, she placed her dish in the sink, thinking she would clean the kitchen last. She had just started up the stairs when her doorbell rang. "OK Ricky, you know who this has to be, right?" she said with a smile and looking toward heaven.

"Good morning Delores. Oh, hi Walter. How are you two?" she said, seeing Delores at the door and her husband standing behind, holding a cake on a cake stand.

"Hi, Jeannie. I hope we didn't awaken you? We just wanted to bring over a nice chocolate cake to help you celebrate that Mutilator case of yours." She turned to Walter who handed her the cake dish. She handed it to Jeannie and then, on cue, told Jeannie how glad she was to have helped solve the case.

"You know Delores, you did it again," Jeanne said in a complementary tone.

Touching her curlers, turning quickly to her husband and then back to Jeannie, Delores said, "Really! Well, what are neighbors for?"

Instead of inviting them in and probably never being able to get rid of them, Jeannie again told Delores that her recollections as a young girl, picking fruit at her aunt's house, really helped. "Do you remember when you said that at times your aunt and uncle had to hire help to pick all the fruit before it spoiled? Well, playing a hunch, we contacted a lot of DIY stores and developed a lead that helped us find the suspect. Good job lady." Jeannie said to a gleaming Delores.

"Oh my God! I can't believe I helped the FBI again. Walter, did you hear that?" Not waiting for an answer from her husband, she told Jeannie they had to run and the two retreated from Jeannie's front door. *Probably off to tell all the neighbors,* Jeannie thought as her cellphone rang on the kitchen counter.

"Loomis," she said without looking at her screen.

"Jeannie, its Farnsworth. Hope I didn't wake you up."

"No, I've been awake for several hours." Jeannie said. "What's up?"

"Did you catch the news this morning?"

"No, in fact I didn't watch it last night either," she replied.

"You know those two juveniles we chased after Munoz decided to lose his head? Well, a student from one of our local high schools reported a conversation he heard those two having in the school's gym. The assholes were planning on doing a Columbine at their high school, but with some remote-controlled bombs added to the mix. Fortunately, this kid reported what he heard to a teacher who didn't dismiss it. She ran it up the chain and it finally reached law enforcement. We hit these two numbskulls 'houses with simultaneous search warrants and found a detailed map, explosives and handguns. But get this. We found an ice pick."

The ride to the San Francisco hospital turned out to be a nice ride. Jeannie had her hair in a ponytail and he had removed the roof section of her Corvette to take in the smells of the bay. She didn't know if Ismail could eat chocolate, but bought some See's candy anyway. *I mean,* she thought, *who can resist See's candy?* She learned from Ismail's wife that he had been moved to a new room and was out of the ICU. Jeannie spent the entire afternoon and late evening hours with his wife while he was in surgery, holding hands and crying together. They hugged when the surgeon told them no major damage was done, and that he would recover with no side effects.

"Hey, I've heard of ways to get out of work, but this takes the cake," Jeannie said as she entered his room, winking at Ismail and giving his wife a hug.

"Hey boss. It's going to take more than one bullet to put me down. I'm USDA choice. I told you."

"God, you are so full of yourself. How do you put up with him?" Jeannie asked, turning to Ismail's wife.

"It isn't easy, I tell you," she replied.

"So, are we taking any heat about Anita's death and the killing of Jerome?" Ismail asked, trying to get more comfortable on his pillow.

"No," Jeannie said. "Almost all of her friends felt it was coming and questioned why she stayed with him as long as she did while being beaten and abused. As for Jerome, the liberal press is not pushing their favorite narrative of a white person killing a black man. Maybe it's because I'm a female, or possibly because Jerome killed his girlfriend. Who knows? The doctor says you'll be getting released in a few days. I want you to take off as much time as you need. You hear me?"

"Yes ma'am. But you know, you can't keep a good man down."

COMING IN FALL 2021

THE FOURTH REICH

A Jeannie Loomis Novel
(Introducing Agent Sean Delaney)

By
Gary J. Rose

Since the collapse of the Third Reich starting with the suicide of Adolf Hitler, anxieties have persisted concerning the possible revival of Nazism and a new Fourth Reich. Germany demolished the Furner bunker so it could not become a shine for the infamous leader, in addition to other sites connected to the Nazis. But even after these measures were taken, Neo-Nazi groups sprang up not only in Germany, but throughout the world.

In the Fourth Reich, Jeannie Loomis reconnects with Interpol agent Delaney. The two previously investigated the planned theft of a religious artifact: the original Ark of the Covenant, supposedly held in a small chapel in Ethiopia. That investigation resulted in disaster for Jeannie. Agent Delaney and Interpol are investigating the world-wide abduction of women in their early twenties, many from the United States. Initially, feeling it may be the act of an international sex trade ring, Delaney reaches out to Jeannie and her team for assistance.

The deeper they delve into the mystery of the missing women; the evidence starts mounting of a sinister group of modern-day Nazis who have continued the work of cloning started by Dr. Josef Mengele in his experiments conducted on Jews in death camps. Through advances in cloning, these modern-day Nazis have set their goal of bringing back their messiah, Adolf Hitler.

www.ingramcontent.com/pod-product-compliance
Lightning Source LLC
Chambersburg PA
CBHW070833020826
48982CB00019B/1063/J

* 9 7 8 1 7 3 4 8 5 2 4 4 8 *